REGIONS BEYOND

Charlotte Strauwald

PublishAmerica
Baltimore

© 2008 by Charlotte Strauwald.
All rights reserved. No part of this book may be reproduced, stored in a retrieval system or transmitted in any form or by any means without the prior written permission of the publishers, except by a reviewer who may quote brief passages in a review to be printed in a newspaper, magazine or journal.

First printing

All characters in this book are fictitious, and any resemblance to real persons, living or dead, is coincidental.

PublishAmerica has allowed this work to remain exactly as the author intended, verbatim, without editorial input.

ISBN: 1-60563-025-X
PUBLISHED BY PUBLISHAMERICA, LLLP
www.publishamerica.com
Baltimore

Printed in the United States of America

DEDICATION

A prayer of thanks: God, thank you for my mom, Margie Shelton. She's a hardworking mom, who loves you and wants her children to love you too. She took me to church every time the door was open, and praised and encouraged me in all my endeavors for you, especially my writing. Please bless her and keep her close to your heart forever.

Acknowledgements

Without the patience and encouragement of my husband, Jack, and my children, Sheri and Tim, this book would not have come to fruition.

Chapter 1

The city of the King shimmered like a green rainbow against the cerulean sky. The two travelers quickened their step. Fired with joy at the summons, the feet of the two angels barely touched the streets of spun gold as they moved forward alongside the river. Zephyrs of perfume floated up from the flowers along the river, but the sweetness of their fragrance didn't compare to the harmonies of praise that echoed in melting music from the palace before them. The travelers followed the river of living water to its source and entered the throne-room. With folded wings and bowed heads, the two angels knelt before the blue robed figure whose penetrating eyes blazed below a crown of white hair. The larger of the two spoke, "You called us, my Lord?"

"Rise Raphael and fair Zephon, and behold my servant." The Lord moved his hand, bringing a gleam from the gold sash across his chest, and opened a vista before them.

An old man rested on his knees. A scent filled the throne-room, pure and refreshing as an alpine meadow in spring; it rose to them from the whispers of the saint. Tears trailed from the man's closed eyes, and his voice trembled with emotion, "Lord, I thank you and praise you for helping me do my part in praying for this young man. Please bring him back, Lord, and show me if I can do anything else to help. By the power invested in me in Christ, I ask that you restrain the satanic forces seeking to destroy the boy. Surround him with angels and protect him. Thank you, Lord. Thank you, Jesus." The man lifted his hands and face toward heaven and continued to pray; a light started in his face with a smile and spread an incandescent glow around him.

The jewel-crusted swords hanging at the angels' sides shimmered in response to the man's prayer until their brilliance filled the throne-room with light. Raphael and Zephon felt the energy surge from their fingertips to the heart of them, and they seemed to grow in size and strength with every word of the man's prayer.

"My servant stands before me on the edge of the abyss," the Lord said in a voice of heart rending tenderness, and nodded toward the old man. He challenges Chaos and Night, on behalf of your charge, Raphael, and yours also, Zephon. Raphael, you must warn the young man, and protect him most of all from himself."

The powerfully built angel dropped to one knee and bowed his golden head. "Your will be done, Lord."

The master turned to the smaller dark-haired angel. "And you, dear Zephon, look out for your charge with diligence and follow Raphael's counsel in all things."

"Yes, my Lord. As you wish." Her wide-set brown eyes turned to the praying servant. "Is he the only one, Lord?"

"No. There are others, but the enemy forces advance, and many more prayer warriors are needed."

Sierra cracked the door of her room and peeked out into the hallway for a sight of Eleanor's friends. "Why did you pick tonight to have one of your parties, Ellie? Your timing stinks worse than Grandma's pig pen." Muttering, she withdrew at the sight of a golden-headed, muscular man accompanied by a small brunette. Back in her room, her eyes fell on the photograph on her nightstand—an eleven-year-old Eleanor stood with her arm around Sierra's shoulders. Sierra frowned and put her hand to her heart. "Sorry, Lord. Help me not to give up on her. Help me to always be grateful for her generosity."

Eleanor never bothered to invite Sierra to her parties anymore. After receiving a polite "No, thank you" the first few months after

Sierra came to live with her, Ellie didn't even trouble to mention them now.

When Sierra moved to Dallas to shorten her commute to the Bible college and the linguistics training school, she intended to live in a dorm room, but her cousin insisted she come live in her plush and roomy apartment. Sierra knew about Ellie's lifestyle and had serious doubts about the arrangement, so she took the decision before the Lord, just as she tried to do with everything in her life. After much prayer, He answered her through her three most trusted earthly counselors—her grandmother, her pastor, and her missions director—that she should live with Ellie. She didn't argue. "Okay, Lord, you know best," had been her reply, but she felt rather like Daniel entering the lion's den. Sierra had chuckled at the thought because her cousin actually looked like a lioness, with her masses of golden blond curly hair and large, almond shaped eyes of honey brown. Sierra prayed the Lord would open those eyes before Eleanor's lifestyle got her into serious trouble.

Eleanor liked fast music, fast cars, and fast men, and she enjoyed the hunt for all three. As a professional cheerleader in the National Football League, she was in the spotlight, partying hard and apparently loving every moment of it. Now Sierra found herself wondering again about God's reason for this living arrangement. After a drunk football player asked her to go to bed with him weeks earlier, she'd felt compelled to stay in her room during the parties, but it was awkward, and tonight it was proving impossible.

"Father in heaven, you know I promised the kids at the Boys' and Girls' Club to help out with their play tonight. They've worked really hard on it, and they're going to be so disappointed if I don't show up. Please help me get out of this apartment without another horrible experience." She pushed a strand of red hair behind her ear and looked at her watch. "I've got to go now. They need me to help set up."

The smell of heavy perfume and spicy food wafted through the air, invading her room even through the closed door. Feeling as though her eardrums would split from the sheer volume of sound, she rubbed her hands on her jeans, then opened the door slightly to check her escape route again. No threatening males appeared. "Thank you, Lord," she whispered, stepped into the hallway, and eased her way towards the front door. At the end of the hall she stopped.

Blocking her path, a man, dressed all in black, moved his long frame into the doorway and surveyed the room full of noisy people. "Another football game, another party," he grumbled to himself. Running a hand through the dark waves of his hair, he scowled at the faces of the Dallas party scene. "What's the point?" He growled, and gulped the last of his drink, then shook his head as though to clear it. "One more double and I won't give a rip."

"Oh no," she whispered, and twisted her hands together, "There's no help for it." Pulling herself to her full height, she took a deep breath and approached the man on tiptoes.

He spun around in a lightning move and caught her wrist in his iron grip as she raised her hand in self-defense. Eyes narrowed, he inspected his captive. A cynical smile turned up one corner of his mouth.

The noisy crowd of people swirled around them and seemed oblivious to Sierra and her captor, but one couple watched them closely. When the small brunette made a move to interfere, the blond giant spoke in warning, "Wait, I'll have a word with him." Zephon waited a moment after Raphael left, then skirted through the crowd, watching Sierra with one eye and searching with the other.

"This party may not be such a bore after all," the dark-haired man said and studied his captive, scanning her from long straight hair to worn running shoes, then gave her a lopsided grin. "You're not a runner; you're a Rossetti painting come to life."

A lava flow moved up Sierra's cheeks, and she lifted her chin, her lips tightening. "And you're rude. Let me go." She insisted and pulled on her hand.

The blond man Sierra had noticed earlier stepped up to her captor and tapped him on the shoulder. "Hey, Josh. You really ought to let the lady go, or you'll be sorry."

Not recognizing the voice, Josh turned his head. He eyed the man's powerful form, saw the resolution in his gray eyes and matched it with his own. "Mind your own business, stranger." All the while he maintained his hold on Sierra's wrist.

She tried to pull her hand away while peering through the crowd, trying to locate the leopard print of Eleanor's gown to no avail. He tightened his grip. "Please, let me go." Twisting her arm, she tried to escape again, but he held her with ease. She looked to the stranger in appeal.

"The name's Ralph," Raphael said, "and the lady's in distress."

"Not as much distress as you're going to be in if you don't mind your own business," Josh said, slurring the words, then turned his back to the stranger as if determined to ignore him. Josh picked up a lock of hair, wrapping it gently round a finger. "Bright as a new copper penny," he said, and his thumb began to stroke the soft underside of her wrist.

Her breath caught in her throat. "You're making a mistake," she protested, "I'm not with these people." While she searched for words to make him understand, his gaze captured hers; shadows of sadness haunted his green eyes, and just for a moment, she wondered how they would look sparkling with joy.

"Wait!" Sierra cried to her assailant when he pulled her into his arms, but he ignored her, molded her body to his, and melted his lips into hers. A shock wave went through Sierra at the touch of his lips on hers, and she started to struggle, then stopped.

"Josh McCabe! Take your hands off my cousin!"

The exclamation startled him into releasing his captive. Sierra jumped away like a coiled spring and darted out the door. With the speed and agility of a trained athlete, Josh moved to stop her but found his path blocked by his determined hostess.

Eleanor grabbed his arms and refused to release him. "Let her go, Josh! She's not your type."

"It's none of your business, Ellie. Get out of my way." Josh moved to pass her, but she ground in her spike heels and stood firm.

"It's very much my business," Eleanor said, "Sierra's my cousin. She's not the kind of girl you're used to."

"Move! She's getting away." He lifted Eleanor to the side and set her out of the way.

"She has no time for you, Josh," Ellie called to his retreating back. "In a few weeks she'll be thousands of miles from here."

"All the more reason to further our acquaintance now," Josh called back as he stepped out the door.

Sierra heard his voice just as she reached the elevator.

"Hey, wait!" He hurried to catch her, but the elevator door closed.

Sierra exhaled audibly, became aware of the fact that she had been holding her breath, and leaned against the wall in an effort to support her shaking body. Her pulse fluttered faster than a hummingbird's wings. "Thank you, Lord, for sending Ellie to rescue me," she whispered.

The elevator stopped, depositing her in the parking garage, and she glanced at her watch. Only ten minutes had passed since her encounter with the green-eyed stranger. As she thought of his embrace, her face blushed, and the heated blood spread through her entire body.

"He has a lot of nerve kissing a total stranger in such a familiar way." She mumbled to herself as she shut the door of her blue Toyota pickup and fastened the seatbelt. "The man's dangerous. Hopefully I'll never set eyes on him again. But what if he's still there when I come back? Lord, please arrange for Josh McCabe to be gone when I come back to Ellie's place."

Eleanor turned to the small brunette who had alerted her to the problem with Josh and Sierra. "Hey, thanks. Wow, that was close." She held out her hand, "I'm Eleanor. I don't think we've met. What's your name?"

The brunette took the offered hand. "Oh. Just call me Phon."

"Fawn. That's a lovely name." Eleanor released the girl's hand slowly and tipped her head to the side with a puzzled expression. "Do I know you?"

"No. I've heard Sierra pr—, uh, mention you a lot though. Speaking of Sierra, do you think Josh will bother her when she returns?" She looked toward the door when she said his name.

Eleanor followed the girl's glance and then scowled. "Not if I can help it." She turned back to Fawn to share her plan, and found herself talking to air. "Well, for Pete's sake. Where'd she go?" She frowned and then shook her head, wondering if the alcohol clouded her brain because something didn't make sense. "Why would Sierra invite a friend to the party when she never attends?" The mystery made Eleanor talk to herself as she threaded her way through the crowd, looking for likely assistants to put her plan for Josh into action.

The frown produced by thoughts of Josh vanished when Sierra arrived at the Boys' and Girls' club and saw the parking lot filling up with cars. The play seemed to be catching a lot of public attention. She was especially happy because Anne, the club director, wanted to raise funds for the club and provide more programs for the young people who frequented the place. Anne had adapted the play *The Duchess of Malfi* to the age of the adolescents. The boys were less than enthusiastic about a play with a female lead, until Sierra pointed out that in the final scenes the stage would be littered with dead bodies.

Sierra arrived backstage to find preparations well underway. Several volunteers in the process of erecting the set greeted her, and she started towards them to lend a hand when a weeping dark-haired girl ran up to her, wringing her hands. The girl grabbed Sierra, and her quivering lips choked back a sob. "I can't do this. I've forgotten every word. Help me, Sierra."

Wrapping an arm around the young woman's shoulders, she smiled in reassurance. "You *can* do this, Jen. You could do it in your sleep. You've known the words for weeks now. Trust me. You're going to be terrific." She gave the girl's shoulder a squeeze.

"Do you really think so?" Jen wiped at the tears that still trickled from her brown eyes, and gulped. "Are you sure? Look, my hands are shaking." She held out trembling fingers.

Sierra took the hands in a firm grasp. "Let's pray, Jen. Okay?" Jen nodded and bowed her head.

"Precious Father, you know how hard Jennifer has worked to learn her part in the play," Sierra prayed in soothing tones. "Please give her peace and confidence that she can do this and help her to do a good job. Please use this to increase her faith in you. For Jesus, amen." Sierra hugged her and rubbed the girl's back. Taking a deep breath, Sierra relaxed her whole body, letting all tension flow out of her. "Did you see how my body relaxed just now, Jen, when I released my breath? I want you to do the same thing." Sierra watched while Jen obeyed her instruction. "Good. I'll be standing right where you can see me all the time. If you forget, look at me and I'll cue you. Okay?"

"Promise?" Jen pushed back her tangled hair, and took another deep breath.

"Yes, I promise, and I'll be praying hard the whole time. You can do this." Sierra took both Jen's shoulders in her hands and stared hard into her face. "You go get into costume and let Marianne do your stage makeup, and when you walk out on that stage, you're going to become the Duchess."

"I'm so glad you're here, Sierra," Jen exclaimed, and gave her a hug before dashing toward the dressing room.

"Oh dear," Sierra said to herself. "Lord, help me remember to tell her I'm leaving in a few days. But not until after the play." Sierra helped to set up the stage and then stood with the team of community service volunteers to watch the play from backstage, assisting in costume and scenery changes, and prompting an occasional forgotten line.

The young people relished the drama and suspense of the Jacobean tragedy, and delivered a spirited performance. Enthusiastic applause erupted after the final curtain. Cheers for Jen's portrayal of the Duchess echoed through the room, and she took another bow, blushing and beaming in pleasure. She rushed up to Sierra after the applause finally died down.

"I was pretty shaky inside at first, but I didn't forget."

"Not a word, and the shakes didn't show at all."

"I just kept praying and taking deep breaths. Thank you, Sierra, for your help. I guess I had a bad case of stage fright."

"You're welcome. I need to thank you too, Jen. The past months have been a joy. I'll treasure their memory always. Especially now that I'm going far away to the mission field."

Jen flung her arms around Sierra. "Don't go. You don't really want to, do you?"

"Of course I do." Sierra returned her hug, then held her away. "Why would you say that?"

"Because every time you mention it, you frown. And you normally smile all the time."

Sierra released the girl and tugged on the collar of her cashmere pullover, struggling to breathe against the smothering weight that settled on her chest like a ten-ton glacier, then forced a smile. "Going to the mission field is serious work, Jen. And I am going. I leave in a few days. Will you pray for me?"

"Yes, every day. But I wish you weren't going." She gave Sierra another hug and then rushed off to join her friends and family.

Sierra watched her go. The doubts about her missionary calling crept in again. Her work with the young people had brought many of them to Christ, and she wanted to watch them grow, but she had to go. She had to. "Help me not to waver, Lord," she whispered.

Zephon felt the surge of power from the prayer at the same moment that she saw the demon of doubt sneaking up on Sierra. Zephon dispatched the deceiver with a well-placed kick and drew her sword to accentuate her point. She watched in satisfaction as the evil worm disappeared. "If only all the obstacles in the path of my charge could be removed with such ease. I wonder if Eleanor was successful in preventing Josh McCabe from hanging around to harass Sierra?"

The music assaulted his ears when Josh opened the door, coming back to the party, which was in full swing now. He scanned the ultra modern, elegant white on white room for his hostess, but she was nowhere in sight.

"Eleanor must be here somewhere," Josh muttered to himself as he searched the large overcrowded living room. "I have a few questions, and I want some answers." He spotted a familiar face. "Hey, KO, have you seen Ellie?"

A large head, set squarely on massive linebacker shoulders, turned in response to his question. "Why, howdy Josh! Great party, ain't it? You're lookin for Ellie, huh? Well, I thought I saw her over yonder a while ago." An arm as large as a tree-trunk pointed vaguely towards the door. "Oh, I see she ain't there anymore. Don't you worry, she'll turn up here somewhere." KO's meaty paw pounded Josh on the shoulder, causing him to wince.

After scouring all the living areas of the apartment and asking several more people, Josh cursed under his breath, "Where the blazes did she get to?" He clenched his fists and resisted the urge to punch someone, then headed towards the bar for another drink, weaving his way through couples. He replied in monosyllables when greetings came his way.

"Josh, ole buddy, what do yah say we blow this place," Raphael said, and clamped his hand in an iron grip on his charge's shoulder. "I know where there's a lot more action."

"I don't think so." Josh turned to face the vaguely familiar voice and discovered Ralph, the stranger from earlier in the evening. Eleanor stood beside him, smiling like a predator who had just caught her prey. She had Jimbo, a huge offensive lineman, on her other side.

"I'm leaving now, and I really want you to come along." The determination in Ralph's voice, the tightening grip on Josh's shoulder, and Jimbo's threatening presence, left little doubt that the captive man would be accompanying them.

Joshua McCabe knew Jimbo outmatched him. Even so, he might have been tempted to try except for Ralph's firm insistence otherwise. "You win this round, Eleanor, but I'll be back," he said, and gave her a mock salute.

CHAPTER 2

Perched in a corner of Eleanor's sunny kitchen, Zephon spread her crystalline wings, reveled in the star's light, and watched her charge, who bustled around the green and white kitchen, humming a praise song as she tied an apron over the gored waistline of her navy dress. Sierra's praises filled Zephon with energy until her own light rivaled the sun's rays.

The rich fragrance of freshly brewed coffee greeted Eleanor when she entered the kitchen, looking rested and beautiful in spite of her late night.

"Thanks, Ellie," Sierra greeted her cousin and poured Eleanor a cup, "for making sure that man was gone when I got back last night."

The lace on Eleanor's peach silk robe fluttered as she pushed back her hair. "You should thank your friend Fawn. She's the one who alerted me to the problem." She took the offered cup, cradled it in both hands, and moved to stand in the window, where her hair reflected the light.

Zephon perked up her ears at the mention of her name and spun eagerly toward Eleanor, but she spotted the saintly nimbus illusion and rolled her eyes.

Sierra turned from the open cupboard with a stack of mixing bowls. She frowned at her cousin. "I don't have a friend named Fawn."

"Really. Are you sure? A sweet little brunette with soft curls to her shoulders and radiant brown eyes. She's about this tall." Eleanor held her hand at chin level.

Sierra shook her head.

"Odd." Eleanor shrugged. "Maybe I misunderstood her. Anyway, it was the least I could do after my guest made such a bore of himself." She sat down her empty cup and chuckled. "Besides, I enjoyed the look on his face when he became aware of the fact that I outsmarted him."

"Do you know him well?" Sierra was surprised when the question came out of her mouth, and she clapped a hand over her mouth, and moaned at the look on her cousin's face.

"Seesee! Are you interested in him?" Eleanor laughed.

"Don't be silly. I don't even know why I asked the question." Flinging her hair over her shoulder, she bent her head over the mixing bowl and punished the pancake batter.

"Maybe I shouldn't have been so quick to come to your rescue last night. Come to think of it, you weren't resisting that kiss very much."

Sierra felt hot color rise into her face as her cousin and her guardian angel watched in fascination. Ducking her head, she busied herself pouring the batter onto the griddle.

"Actually, I don't blame you. Josh is a terrific kisser." Eleanor lifted her eyebrows and watched her cousin's face as she made this statement.

Sierra swung to face her. "You've kissed him!" Her eyes were wide.

"Ha!" Ellie whooped. "I knew it." She danced around the kitchen, clapping her hands.

Sierra swatted at Eleanor with the spatula, a sheepish smile on her face. "You've never kissed him, have you, you rat? Confess or I'll burn your pancakes." She laughed at her cousin and turned back to the stove.

Zephon giggled, and clapped her hands.

"Okay, I'll admit I've never kissed him, if you'll admit you're curious about him," Eleanor said. Her eyes sparkled with gold facets almost the exact shade as her hair.

"I won't admit anything of the kind. It's ready. Sit." Sierra shoveled the pancakes from the grill and handed Ellie a plate, then placed another plate on the table and took a seat. Clasping her hands, she waited for Eleanor to bow her head. When Sierra came to live there, she had bargained her cooking skills for the privilege of praying over their meals, hoping that sharing her faith in God in prayer would lead Ellie to the Lord. "Precious Father in heaven, thank you for this your day when we are blessed with the privilege of coming together with other Christians to worship you. Lord, I pray that many people will open their hearts today and accept your son as their savior so that there will be great rejoicing in heaven. And Father, please send out lots of spiritually mature Christian workers to your harvest fields today, especially to the regions beyond, where knowledge of Jesus hasn't reached. For your glory Father, because I love you. And Lord, thank you for this food. Please bless it to our bodies to help keep us healthy. Amen."

The prayer sent joy and light racing through Zephon, and she felt ready to burst with happiness and battle a host of demon attackers.

Sierra poured homemade blueberry syrup on her pancakes, then passed the jar to her cousin. The sun streaming in the windows bathed the breakfast nook in a cheerful brightness.

"You know, Seesee, these pancakes are scrumptious. I need to get the recipe from you before you leave, but they'll never turn out this good for me." All the sparkle had vanished from Eleanor's eyes when she looked at her cousin. "I'm going to miss you when you're gone."

"I know. I'm going to miss you too."

"Why do you have to go so far away?" Eleanor repeated a much-asked question.

"Please, Ellie, try to understand. You know it's been my goal since we were kids. I have to finish the work my mom and dad started."

"But, are you sure you're doing it for the right reasons, Cous? I mean, aren't you supposed to have a calling or something? Are you sure you're not motivated by guilt?"

"Stop it, Ellie! I know God wants me to do this." Her hand came up to tug the collar of her dress and she stared at her plate, her forkful of pancakes forgotten.

"Okay, okay, don't get all angry about it. I just don't ever remember you talking about being a missionary until after our parents were killed in the avalanche. Are you sure you aren't still blaming yourself?"

"I don't want to talk about that." Sierra rose from the table and carried her plate to the sink.

"It wasn't your fault, Seesee."

"They were looking for me." She didn't turn around.

"You were only eight years old, and you got lost."

"I should've paid more attention to the signs," Sierra said quietly. The running water that almost drowned her soft words transformed to the thunder of crashing snow in Sierra's mind. Blinking away the moisture that threatened to escape her eyes, she silenced the water and stiffened her shoulders. "Please try to understand Ellie. I know God wants me to do this." Hearing herself repeating the assurance, she felt the icy claws of doubt slide over her heart.

Zephon saw the small demon of doubt trying to sink its claws into Sierra, and her sword sang from its sheath. "Release her and return to the slimy pit from which you sprang." The demon eluded the blade's sharp edge and vanished into black mist.

"Whatever." Eleanor shrugged her shoulders. "I can see there's no point arguing with you." She sipped her coffee in silence for a few minutes, studying her cousin, and then a glint of mischief brightened her eyes. "There's a lot of mystery attached to Josh McCabe. He's the kicker for Dallas, but no one knows exactly where he learned to kick. There are lots of rumors. Some people think he played soccer growing up in the jungle or some strange place like that."

Zephon listened with great interest, curious about Raphael's charge, and aware that knowledge creates power.

"He grew up in a jungle?" Sierra stopped clearing the table. "Were his parents in the military? Why did they live in the jungle?"

"I don't know. The gals in the dressing room didn't mention any details about that. He's only been in Dallas for a year or two and he's a very private person." Eleanor's eyes narrowed like a cat ready to pounce. "You're really intrigued by him, aren't you? You know, if you really want to learn about Josh, you could go to the source. Ask him."

Sierra looked up. "I an not intrigued, and I will not ask him. In fact, I hope I never see him again. He's nothing but a rude, overbearing bully. No, no way. I'm not interested in Mr. McCabe. Besides, I can't take a chance on falling in love with a non-Christian."

"Why would it be such a bad thing? Maybe he could stop you from going off into that jungle, thousands of miles away from everyone who loves you. Especially Grandma Charlotte. She's old, you know. What if she dies?"

Sierra set the dishes in the sink and turned tear filled eyes to her cousin. "Please stop."

Eleanor hung her head. "I'm sorry. That was mean of me. But really, maybe Josh is a Christian."

"I don't think so," Sierra said, shaking her head. "Or, if he is, he certainly isn't a very happy Christian."

"I don't know why he'd be unhappy. He's one of the most gorgeous guys I've ever seen. Those deep, dark green eyes are really something with his dark hair. But I think you noticed that. You know, I bet he comes over here today."

Chapter 3

Raphael stood with sword drawn, holding the demons of anger, impatience, and defiance at bay; their tentacles reattached themselves to Josh in spite of the angel's slashing blows. Only the prayers of the faithful servants kept his arm strong enough to fend them off.

"I hate answering machines." Josh slammed down the phone, ran a hand through his hair and stared blindly at the green and tan décor of his condo. The last two weeks would have tried the patience of a very long-suffering person, and Josh had lost that virtue long ago. Returning to Eleanor's apartment the day after the party, he had found no one home. Intense workouts and practices in preparation for play-off games, combined with two away games, had consumed most of his time, but he still found himself distracted by memories of long red hair and turquoise blue eyes. With every thought of her came the echo of Ralph's voice warning him to resist temptation and let Sierra go or be sorry. That advice just strengthened his resolve and made him more determined to see her again. Plagued by Eleanor's claim that Sierra would be leaving town shortly, he called daily, only to be frustrated by the electronic device.

"She won't find it that easy to ignore me now that the season's over. I'll haunt the place until she shows up." He grabbed his denim jacket and headed for the door.

The ring of the phone halted him with his hand on the knob.

"Josh here," he growled, "Make it quick." One foot began to tap the floor. A deep, familiar chuckle on the other end of the line jolted his manners back into place. "Uh, Dr. Cook. Hello. How are you?" The tapping foot stopped, and he ran his hand through his hair and sighed, grimacing at his rudeness.

Raphael smiled at the sound of the prayer warrior's voice. With renewed strength, he sent the demons fleeing, while listening with heightened interest to the conversation.

"I'm wonderful, Josh," Dr. Cook said. "I won't ask you the same question. I can tell by the tone of your voice that something's got you riled. I'll trust the Lord to work it out for you."

"Thanks, Dr. Cook. I haven't heard from you in a long time." A bloody vision jumped into his mind—his father's body full of native spears—and his chest constricted as though wrapped by an anaconda. "Is something wrong? Are my folks all right?"

"They're fine, son. I didn't mean to alarm you."

Josh filled his lungs with oxygen and sank into a leather chair with a sigh. For long moments he heard nothing on the other end of the phone, and he knew Dr. Cook was praying. Prayer was like breathing to the mission director, continuous and essential.

"You're still carrying a heavy load, Joshua. I can hear it in your voice. It's been too long now. Let it go. Do you want to pray with me?"

"No!" Josh snapped, and then clamped his mouth shut.

"Your parents are one of the reasons I'm calling. I spoke with your father this morning. He said you're coming out to Irian."

"That's right," Josh said, in control again. "I'm leaving in a few days."

A deep chuckle came from Dr. Cook. "Wonderful, my boy, that's wonderful."

Josh smiled wryly, felt the pain in his chest ease, and shook his head. "You know, Dr. Cook, every time you chuckle like that it means you know something I don't know, and I'm afraid to find out what."

"I think you're going to like this 'what' very much. Oh yes, very much indeed." He sounded amused. "Can you come to my office this afternoon? I have a special favor to ask of you, and also someone I want you to meet."

"Sure. What time?"

"About three o'clock."

"No problem. I'll be there." Josh nodded and smiled to himself. "I wonder what he's up to?"

"A lot of praying for one thing. You should try it." Raphael answered silently.

Dr. Cook's voice summoned so many good memories from Josh's childhood. As director of the mission organization through which his parents worked, Dr. Cook played an important part in his life for as long as he could remember. In all those years Josh never once heard Dr. Cook raise his voice or have a harsh word to say to anyone. He'd been like a second father to Josh, coming to his soccer games when Josh's father was out of town and taking the time to show him how to improve his soccer skills, counseling him through all the adjustments to living in the United States when Josh's family returned from the field. Josh loved him.

"It'll be good to see him again," Josh said aloud. He looked at his watch. "Three this afternoon. That gives me time to see if I can track down a certain redhead." He shrugged into his jacket and headed out the door.

Shaking his head, Raphael followed, wondering at the stubbornness of his charge.

When the doorbell rang, Eleanor frowned in exasperation and looked down at the pink silk of her nightgown and open robe. "For heaven's sake. I just finished my nails." She blew on the glossy coral tips while walking barefoot across the plush white carpet. The bell rang again. "I'm coming, wait a second." Grasping the knob, she tried to avoid smearing the wet polish. Opening the door with the skill of a contortionist, she stood facing Josh. With a smile and a lift of her perfectly arched eyebrows, she greeted him, "Well, you took your time. I expected to see you banging down the door the day after the party." Waving him in, she stepped aside.

"I was here," Josh growled, "No one was home. And I've been

calling for two weeks. Why hasn't anyone returned my calls?"

Raphael followed close beside Josh, aware that the danger to his charge escalated when they entered Eleanor's apartment.

"Have you now? You do have a bad case." She started to smile but stopped when his brows lowered over darkening eyes. "Actually, I've been out of town for two weeks myself." She frowned at her hands. "I just got back this morning only to find my manicurist is sick. Oh! these nails are such a mess."

"Is Sierra here?"

"Not much for small talk, are you?" Eleanor spun around, diaphanous silk swirling, and returned to her spot on the white velvet sofa.

"I don't have time for it. You said she'd be leaving in a few weeks. The few weeks are almost up. Or was that just a lie to make me lose interest?" He followed and stood over her like a smoking mountain.

Eleanor raised her chin and her eyes widened, then narrowed. "Back off, Josh. I wasn't lying, and I'm insulted you'd think so." She took his hand and kissed the knuckles. "Besides, I don't want to be your enemy. We're friends, aren't we?" She patted the cushion next to her. "Sit down."

"I'd rather stand." He removed his hand from her grasp and put it in the pocket of his jacket, rubbing the knuckles against the rough denim. He backed away a few steps, considering her question. "All right, I'm sorry. I've had a difficult two weeks, and I'm taking it out on you. Although at least part of it's your fault. You did interfere with Sierra and me at the party."

"I had something to do with that also," Raphael mused.

"Yes, I did," Eleanor said, and frowned at his hand that stayed securely in his pocket. "It's an old habit from our childhood. Seesee is more like a sister than my cousin. I'm older and bigger than she is, so I've always run interference for her. Besides, it was obvious she needed protection."

Josh pressed his lips together and ran a hand through his hair. "I'll admit I did come on a little strong."

"To Sierra, that wasn't a little strong. That was a full blown hurricane." Eleanor grimaced at him.

He stalked to the white marble fireplace, leaned an arm on it, and turned to face her. "What the blazes was she doing at that kind of party if she doesn't want guys to come on to her?"

"She wasn't at the party. No, wait." She stopped him with a raised hand when he started to interrupt. "Let me explain. Seesee lives here with me but she doesn't attend my parties. She usually stays in her room. She only came out of her room because she promised to help out another college student, or was it that kid's club place. She's an habitual volunteer, you know." Eleanor stood, fastened the sash of her robe, and walked toward the kitchen. Josh followed and she pulled out a chair for him. "Sit down, Josh. I promise not to bite. Coffee?" She stepped to the counter and poured herself a cup.

"No, thanks. Who gave her the nickname, and what's she studying?" Josh sat on the opposite side of the table from her, and the tension seemed to drain out of him.

Sensing the change, Raphael relaxed, replaced his sword in its scabbard, folded his arms, and listened with interest to the conversation.

Eleanor stirred cream and sugar into her porcelain cup, took a sip, and sat down before answering. "I get credit for the name. I was three when she was born. I couldn't say Sierra, so I called her Seesee. This conversation reminds me of the one I had with my cousin the morning after the party." She gave him a Cheshire cat grin and didn't hesitate to fabricate. "She was curious about you too."

As Josh registered this bit of information, Eleanor watched a slow smile spread across his face, becoming a full-blown grin.

The transformation amazed her. "You know, that's a great smile. You should use it more often. It really is too bad my cousin is so stubborn. You two would make a gorgeous couple. Why she won't listen to reason, I don't know. It's really sad. She's so hardheaded and fixated. She reminds me of our old dog, Rags, worrying a bone and refusing to let go of it."

"What're you talking about?"

Eleanor shrugged and shook her head; her full lips turned down. "She wants to be a missionary, and I just know it's a guilt thing from our childhood. She's going thousands of miles away to live with natives in some unheard of place," she explained, "and it's breaking my heart because I won't be there to run interference for her when she gets into trouble." She sat her coffee down slowly when she saw the blood drain from his face.

With a violent movement he pushed back from the table, jolting Eleanor's coffee onto the white lace tablecloth, stood up and stumbled to the door.

"Josh, what's wrong? Are you ill?"

Raphael hadn't seen the demons of fear and despair approaching. Their claws sank into Josh and fought to hang on even against the punishing blows from the angel blade.

Josh turned stricken eyes to her and stared as though in a daze. "It's like a nightmare that won't go away. This can't be happening again. Not again." The door slammed as he hurried out as if fleeing for his life.

"Wait! Don't you want to wait for Sierra to come home?" Eleanor's last question filled the empty room. "Well, for heavens sake," she said, staring at the closed door. "What got hold of him?"

Josh pulled into a parking space and turned off the ignition; staring at the shiny black hood of his new truck, he tried to quiet the turmoil in his mind. He took a deep breath, oblivious even to the new car scent that usually soothed him, and ran a hand through his hair before glancing at his watch. He had been driving around for hours before heading to Dr. Cook's office for their three o'clock appointment. He rested his head on the steering wheel. "A missionary," he groaned. "That's rich. She wants to go off into the wilderness and get herself killed. What are you trying to do to me?" He looked toward heaven and laughed bitterly.

In the backseat, Raphael just shook his head. "I did try to warn you."

Chapter 4

Legions of shadows clouded Josh's eyes as he walked into Dr. Cook's office. His old friend came forward, clasped Josh's hand in both of his and smiled, lifting Josh's spirit as only Dr. Cook could.

"It's good to see you, son." He looked into the young man's face, saw the struggle, and sent a prayer for peace toward Heaven. "I'm glad to see you're still in excellent physical condition. That's good. Come, sit down and I'll tell you about the favor I mentioned on the phone."

Raphael entered after Josh, bowed to Dr. Cook's guardian, Ariel, and removed his hand from his sword, knowing the foe dared not enter the powerful angel's presence.

Josh took a seat in the comfortable, softly lighted, oak and leather office and glanced around. "This place hasn't changed since I was a boy." He and his parents, big brother Michael, and little sister Sarah, spent long hours in this room. Making plans for missionary trips, his parents held deep conversations with Dr. Cook, his father's hair so dark and his mother's glinting russet in the light, their heads bent over the missionary director's desk. Michael, Sarah, and he played on one side of the room where lots of children's toys, games and books were kept on hand to keep little hands and minds busy, while the adults discussed the best strategies to evangelize unreached people of the world. The memory of their enthusiastic voices and images replayed softly like an echo in his mind. Michael's blue eyes gleamed in triumph as he jumped a row of Josh's men on the checkerboard, while Sarah's amber curls bounced in rhythm to the rocking motion of her favorite chair. Josh closed his eyes.

Dr. Cook sat behind his well-worn desk, hands folded on a capacious middle. Moisture glazed his warm brown eyes and revealed the love he felt for the young man as he watched the sorrowful expressions flitting across Josh's face. "I'm the one who has changed, son," he said. "I'm not getting any younger, and I've been told by my doctor I must slow down, and I'm endeavoring to do so. Now, don't look so alarmed. But, that's why I need your help."

"I'll be glad to do anything I can for you, Dr. Cook. You know that."

"I do, Josh. Actually, I think you may enjoy doing this particular good deed very much. There is a young lady who is going to the field for the first time. As you know, I don't like our first time missionaries to travel alone. I had planned to make the trip myself, but due to my doctor's orders, I won't be able to go. I would consider it a personal favor and great blessing to me if you could take my place."

"I suppose I could postpone my trip to visit my parents."

"Oh no. That's what made me think of asking for your help. You see, Sierra is going to Irian Jaya."

"What…" Josh said, and sat up straight in his chair, wondering if he'd heard correctly.

"You see that's why this is so wonderful. Sierra is going there and so are you."

"Did you say Sierra?" Every muscle in his body tensed; his hands tightened on the chair arms, and he prepared to bolt for the door, hoping there could be two missionaries with the same name.

"Yes, Sierra Evans."

Raphael digested this information and realized that his job had just become harder.

Josh swallowed forcefully and decided he should get up and get out of there as fast as his legs could carry him, but the reluctant limbs refused to move. He wanted as little to do with missionaries as possible. He hadn't even been to visit his parents in three years. But he knew if he didn't go with Sierra, Dr. Cook might try to go and make himself very sick, and Josh couldn't risk it. Taking a grip on his emotions, Josh forced himself to relax.

His old friend didn't seem to notice Josh's consternation at the identity of the missionary. "You know your parents need help on the translation project they're working on, and we're very excited about Sierra's potential. She's an amazing young woman. She's multi-lingual, some would say a linguistic genius. Your parents are looking forward to having her join them." He stopped listing her accomplishments and looked at the opening door. "Sierra, come in, come in. Join us."

From his relaxed position on the corner of Dr. Cook's desk, Raphael waved to Zephon and motioned her to join him. Zephon bowed to the angel behind Dr. Cook and then hastened to accept, glad of the opportunity to be near Dr. Cook, the old prayer warrior whose many petitions for her charge had strengthened Zephon's arm against the demon forces.

Standing, Josh turned as Sierra entered the room. She was clothed in a simple sea green dress, and her hair fell in silken waves to her waist. Her tanned skin glowed, and the red hair shot sparks even in the room's soft lighting. His hands clenched. He cautioned himself to remember her chosen profession; at the same time he wondered why this was happening to him.

Dr. Cook had moved from behind his desk to meet her. She shook his extended hand and than turned to face Josh.

She gasped and touched her heart.

Josh stretched his lips into the semblance of a smile and nodded without saying a word, but the muscle in his jaw ached from tension.

"You two know each other?" Dr. Cook looked from one to the other, and his eyes widened. Then a smile started in his eyes and moved to encompass his whole face.

"Yes. No," was Sierra's confused reply. "I mean—" She tore a horrified gaze from Josh's face and turned to Dr. Cook. "We haven't actually been formally introduced."

Josh choked back a snort that drew his old friend's gaze and caused a lifted brow.

"I see," Dr. Cook said, "Well, we can remedy that immediately. Sierra Evans, I'd like to introduce you to a young man who's like a son to me, Joshua McCabe."

Like a robot, she turned. "Mr. McCabe," she said, and extended her hand, but the distrust on her face said she wanted to run away.

He took her hand reluctantly, hearing a litany of warning in his mind; it echoed like a voice in a tunnel, endlessly repeating her profession.

"Sit down, sit down. Now, let's get busy. We have lots of plans to make." Dr. Cook returned to his chair behind the well-polished desk, looked at the two of them and chuckled.

For the first time in his life, Josh felt anger at the mission director.

"Now, I've made arrangements for the two of you to fly out of Dallas/Fort Worth at 6:15 this coming Thursday morning. Will that work for you?"

"Excuse me, Dr. Cook," Sierra said. Her voice sounded choked, and she put a hand to her throat. "Did you say the two of us?" She glanced up at Josh and then back to Dr. Cook. "I thought *you* were to accompany me to Irian Jaya?"

"I'm sorry, my dear. I'm afraid I'm to be denied that pleasure. Orders from my doctor."

"Are you ill?" She leaned forward, placing her hand on his desk.

"No, no. It's nothing to be alarmed about. I just must slow down."

"But why is Mr. McCabe going?" She glanced at Josh when he moved restlessly.

A frown drew his dark brows together. He pushed the hair back from his brow and said, "I was planning a trip to Irian anyway. When Dr. Cook discovered my plans, he asked me to take his place."

"But why?" Sierra felt she was missing something. She couldn't understand why Josh McCabe would want to visit an unheard of place like Irian Jaya.

"Because James and Elizabeth McCabe, the missionaries you're going to work with, are my parents." He watched her face mirror astonishment, then horror. He realized that she was not happy about the turn of events. Her displeasure wasn't surprising. He hadn't exactly been Mister Cordiality. But she wasn't the only one upset by the plan; a missionary was the last person on earth he wanted to be attracted to, and now they were traveling together and then living in the same house. Josh's runaway thoughts hit a wall, and he knew this was one visit he had to cut short. He resolved to just accompany her there, spend a few days with his parents, and then get the heck out of there. Satisfied with his plan, he turned his attention back to the meeting.

The angels listened to the travel plans with great interest. Zephon's hand slipped to the hilt of her sword when she heard the change in plans.

With eyes like warning signs of neon blue, Sierra stared at Dr. Cook, hoping he would deny the statement.

The mission director smiled, and a chuckle came rumbling from deep in his chest. "Yes, my dear, Josh was raised as a missionary kid too. Since he was two years old that is," he explained in a calm and soothing voice. "Josh and his parents are very old and dear friends of mine."

Stunned into silence, Sierra sat almost in shock, far from soothed, while Dr. Cook and her soon to be traveling companion made all the arrangements for their departure and the shipment of supplies in route to his parents. She had a lot of questions, but they were for Dr. Cook's ears alone.

"Well, I think that about covers everything," Josh commented, rising from his chair. "I don't know about you, but I'm starving. I seem to have skipped lunch. I think I'll get some dinner. Would you care to join me, Sierra?" He felt like dropkicking his tongue the instant the words left his mouth, and he reminded himself that he wasn't going to get involved. He opened his mouth to retract the offer.

"No thank you, Mr. McCabe," Sierra whispered through stiff lips. She glanced his way to find him frowning even more, an angry grimace distorted his face.

"I'll be calling you." He jerked his eyes away from her to find Dr. Cook observing them closely, joy twinkling in his eyes. The unfamiliar anger surged into Josh's throat and he choked out. "I'll be here in a few days to help load those supplies."

"Wonderful, son," came his enthusiastic reply, "I'll see you then."

The office door closed behind Josh, and Dr. Cook turned his gentle gaze on Sierra. "I can see, my dear, that you're very distressed by the change in your travel arrangements."

"Well, I..." She stumbled over the words to explain her attitude.

"It's all right. I think I understand. I gather that you and Josh have met previously, and perhaps that meeting gave you a bad first impression."

Sierra found it impossible to tell him what she thought of Josh. She wasn't even sure herself. But there was one thing she felt compelled to find out. "Dr. Cook, is Josh a Christian?"

His white head nodded as if he had expected her question, and a smile lit his face like an angel's. "Oh yes, my dear. Josh is most definitely a Christian. I had the great privilege of leading Josh to the Lord when he was seven years old."

"Then why is he...?" she begin, but could not find it in her heart to tell the wonderful old Christian warrior what was happening in the life of his friend.

"I know, dear. You don't need to explain. Josh is having a very difficult time right now, and he blames God. This young man that you see is not the real Josh. He's simply releasing his anger in the only way he has allowed himself."

Sierra left the office, headed for her faded blue truck, and resolution straightened her spine. "Well, he has no right to release it on me. I won't be his victim."

Chapter 5

"I'm getting really tired of talking to this machine." Josh's voice entered the room with eerie clarity. "Where are you, and why haven't you returned my calls?" The answering machine clicked and whirred as it rewound the tape.

"Oh my, he does sound angry, Seesee. Didn't you tell Josh we would be at Grandma Charlotte's for two days?"

"It's none of Mr. McCabe's business, Ellie. I don't need his permission to go out of town." Tugging on the collar of her dark turquoise turtleneck, she carried her coffee to the living room, kicked off her shoes and curled into the corner of the sofa, clutching the cup beneath her nose like she could escape into its fragrant depths.

Zephon nodded in agreement and followed her charge from the kitchen, moving to a spot by the hearth.

"Sierra, I'm surprised at you," Ellie said, and clicked her tongue in disapproval. "This whole thing of traveling with Josh has really put you out of sorts. Try to look on the bright side. He's terribly good-looking and might be fun, given half a chance." Ellie yawned, stretched, rearranged her green velvet caftan around her legs and relaxed into the sofa.

"He isn't *that* good looking, and I don't want to find out that he's fun," Sierra muttered into her steaming cup. She winced when she saw her cousin's eyebrows raise with interest.

"That disturbs you, to think that you could like him, doesn't it?"

Ellie said. The corners of her lips curved upwards.

"A lot of things disturb me lately. Did Gran look well to you?" Changing the subject, she looked into her cup, refusing to meet Eleanor's eyes.

"She has lost weight, not that she had much to lose. Good heavens, she's almost eighty years old. You can't expect her to live forever."

Sierra sat her cup down and turned a tear-filled gaze to her. "How can you talk that way? As if you don't even care."

"Don't be ridiculous." Eleanor's eyes flashed. "I love Gran as much as you do, but I'm a realist. People get old, and then they die." The stricken look on Sierra's face brought instant remorse. "Seesee, I'm sorry. I know how you feel about Gran. She's all the family we have." Eleanor reached over and folded her cousin in a hug, then patted her back. "She'll be all right. You'll see. You know she's got to live for a long time yet, so she can brag about her granddaughter, the missionary."

A little smile tugged up the corners of Sierra's mouth. "Gran is very happy for me. I think she's more excited than I am." Shocked at her own words, she gulped, hoping Eleanor didn't notice. "Being with her just brought back so many happy memories."

"She was always there for us," Eleanor said, with a faraway look. "When our parents were killed in the accident, I shudder to think what would have happened to us if not for Gran."

"How she ever coped with an eight and an eleven year old when she herself was in her sixties is beyond me. We must have been a handful."

"Not me, I was a perfect angel." Eleanor patted her hair.

Zephon rolled her eyes at the terminology.

"Huh! I remember one summer afternoon," Sierra said. "I think you were twelve. That's right, it was the second summer after we came to live with Gran. You were bored and talked me into playing dress up, pretending Rags was our little sister. We raided Gran's closet and dressed Rags in what we thought was Gran's oldest dress and hat because she never wore them. Of course the dress wasn't made to fit an old English sheep dog."

Eleanor laughed in delight. "Well, everything was fine until Rags got tired of the game and jumped out of the red wagon and started running. We chased her all over the yard trying to persuade her to get back in her 'baby carriage'."

From her perch on the fireplace hearth, Zephon smiled at the story.

With a flip of her hand, Sierra tossed her hair over her shoulder and laughed at the memory. "I'll never forget the look on Gran's face when she saw her best dress and hat hanging in tatters on her old sheep dog's back."

"I thought for sure we were in for it. My knees shook so hard that my socks fell down."

"I know. Remember Gran told us later she didn't know whether to laugh or to cry. I also remember you stepped forward and told Gran the whole thing was your idea." Sierra smiled at her cousin.

"Only because it was true."

"You were always running interference for me, Ellie."

A velvet clad shoulder shrugged. "Old habits are hard to break." Her golden eyes dimmed. "I won't be able to do it now."

"I know. I'm going to miss you."

Never one to be morose for long, Eleanor quickly changed the subject. "I doubt you'll have time to miss me very much; you'll probably be spending half your time just fending off advances from Josh."

"That's what I'm afraid of." Sierra caught her bottom lip between her teeth. She turned away to gaze out the window where waves of puffy coral clouds floated in an ocean of dark blue sky under the setting sun.

"Honestly, Seesee, what are you afraid of? You go all stiff as uncooked pasta whenever I mention him."

"It would never work for us, Ellie." She took a sip from her cup and sighed.

"Why not for heavens sake? He's got everything. He's gorgeous, he's intelligent, he's successful in his career, and he's eligible." She ticked off on her fingers as she counted Josh's attributes.

"And he's a Christian." Sierra added to the list.

"He is?" Ellie turned to look at Sierra with lifted eyebrows, then she frowned. "But then what's the problem?"

"You wouldn't have known he was a Christian if I hadn't told you, now would you?"

"No," Ellie admitted.

"That's the problem," Sierra said, "Ellie, remember what Gran used to say 'Don't just tell me, show me'. A real Christian is one in deed, not just in name only. If I ever marry, it must be someone who truly loves the Lord, and is living for him, not against him."

Ellie's frown deepened, and she shook her head. "But you said he's a Christian."

"A Christian with a hardened heart, dear cousin, is not the kind of man I want."

"Brava!" Zephon cheered, and her dark curls bounced.

"Okay fine. It sounds like you've made up your mind that he's wrong for you. So just tell him you're not interested."

"It's not that simple. I have to work with his parents for a whole year. I don't want to offend them by snubbing their son." Sierra sank further into the sofa cushions and gazed into her lukewarm cup.

Eleanor pursed her lips. "You're not fooling me, darling cousin. Since we were kids you've never been able to look me in the face and tell a lie."

"I'm not lying," Sierra said, cheeks flushing.

Eleanor snorted in a very unladylike manner. "You're not being totally honest either. I think you're already in love with Josh McCabe." She stared her cousin down.

Zephon's eyes snapped open, and she looked from Eleanor to her charge.

Sierra nearly choked on her coffee. "That's ridiculous. I've only seen him twice in my life. I couldn't possibly be in love with him. I'm surprised at you, 'Miss Realistic,' for even suggesting such a thing."

The outburst prompted a ripple of laughter from Eleanor. "There is such a thing as love at first sight. Remember Gran's stories about Grampa Jed? They fell in love the instant they met."

"Are you forgetting the rest of the story, Ellie? Grandpa Jed was not a Christian, but Gran was in love and too blind to realize the truth. They were married for fifteen years before Grampa really surrendered his life to the Lord. Gran said those first fifteen years were the most difficult of her life. I don't want to spend fifteen years of my life swinging from joy to misery like our grandmother did."

"For someone as special as Josh, it might be worth it," Eleanor replied.

"Are you sure you're not enamored with Mr. McCabe?"

Eleanor studied the nails on her left hand. "That would be a total waste of my time and energy. If you'd been a bug on the wall when he came by the other day, you'd believe me." She looked at Sierra. "It's you he wants."

"How absurd, you're talking nonsense. He was just so drunk at the party that he couldn't see straight." Sierra leaned forward to set her empty cup down and then pushed her hair over her shoulder.

"Huh uh." Eleanor shook her head. "He's obviously smitten with you, Seesee. That's why he keeps calling and that's why he's so angry."

"I really doubt that, Ellie. He's probably just calling to confirm our travel plans."

"Well, why don't you call him back and find out?"

"I plan to." She tugged on her collar again and swallowed. "I just wanted to relax and catch my breath for a few minutes. Could we just drop the subject?"

Ellie shrugged a shoulder and gazed out the window at the city lights.

Sierra stood, picked up her cousins cup, and went to the kitchen to refill them, before returning to her former position.

As companionable silence enfolded them, they sipped their coffee and enjoyed the respite from the long drive home from their grandmother's house. Into the quiet came the melodic chime of Eleanor's doorbell.

Sierra started to rise again, but Eleanor beat her to it with a wave of her hand. "No. Stay there. It's my turn to get up." Adjusting the belt of her caftan, she opened the door.

Josh stood in the hallway with his hand raised to ring the bell again. "Hello, Ellie, it's about time. Is Sierra here?"

Eleanor stood transfixed, aware of very little but the tall stranger beside Josh. With an effort of will, she tore her eyes from the kindest face she had ever seen. "What? Oh, yes. She's here. Please come in." She stepped aside in invitation and closed the door behind them; her eyes fixed on the stranger's broad flannel covered back. Like an ant drawn to sugar, she followed the sandy-headed man into the living room.

"Hello, Mr. McCabe." Sierra glanced his way. She had been curled into the corner of the couch, her feet tucked under her, but as they entered the room, she uncurled, placed her bare feet on the carpet, and stood up, resisting the urge to run to her room.

Josh's gaze followed her motion. He shoved his hands into the pockets of his black leather jacket and clenched his fists. "Sierra and Eleanor Evans, this is Edward Thomas." He nodded toward the other man. "Ed's a good friend of Dr. Cook, and he's helping me load the boxes of supplies and transport them to the airport."

Zephon waved to Raphael and Ed's guardian, Ramiel, who had his hand on his sword and a watchful eye on Eleanor. Zephon frowned at Eleanor who shadowed Ed, thinking her behavior odd, even for Eleanor.

"I'm pleased to meet you." Sierra greeted him and extended her hand, then she tilted her head and asked, "Are you a student at the seminary? You look very familiar to me."

Ed nodded his head while unbuttoning his quilted flannel shirt to reveal a cross emblazoned t-shirt. Yes, I'm a student. I'm graduating this year actually."

Sierra cast a casual glance in her cousin's direction and found Eleanor staring in fascination at Ed.

"Hello, you must be Eleanor." Ed had turned, as if summoned by the stare, and took her outstretched hand. Gold eyes locked with blue. He continued to hold her hand as if unaware that it was still in his grasp until Josh cleared his throat. Ed swallowed hard, dropped Eleanor's hand, took a step back, and crossed his arms over his chest.

"Are you sisters?" he stuttered. "You don't look like each other at all." His voice cascaded down to the last word, and he fell silent.

Sierra watched her cousin blush and fumble for words. She'd never seen Eleanor at a loss for words, especially in front of a man. "Actually, we're cousins. Our fathers were brothers." She had to smile at the thought that she got to run a little interference for Ellie this time. "We don't look alike because Eleanor looks like her maternal grandmother, and I look like mine." Thinking her cousin would be more comfortable with a change of subject, Sierra asked, "Mr. Thomas, are you studying for the ministry?"

"Yes, I am." Ed tore his eyes away from Eleanor. "Lord willing, I'll be pastor of a church someday. And please call me Ed."

"That's wonderful. Isn't that wonderful, Ellie?"

"A pastor...oh," came Eleanor's soft reply, and her brows drew together.

Joy filled Sierra's heart and illumined her smile. She realized that this soft-spoken man of God could be the answer to her prayers for her cousin. She had never seen Eleanor so taken by a man before. She wanted to shout, "Praise the Lord!"

Josh watched Sierra's face light up, and his mouth twisted as the green eyes turned glacial. "Hey, I hate to rush you people, but I have a plane to catch in less than twenty-four hours. Do you want to show me where your boxes are?"

Chapter 6

The bedclothes lay twisted in tangled confusion around Josh's body. Moonlight slanted through the blinds casting bars across his sleeping form. He fought to escape entrapment, but not from the shadow prison.

The dream came again. He was at the party with Sierra in his grasp, and the stranger, Ralph, tapped him on the shoulder. Josh tried to ignore him, but he persisted, and Sierra escaped. Josh tried to follow. With one hand on Josh's shoulder, the stranger prevented him from catching her, exploding Josh's anger like jolted nitro. Josh swung around, fist raised, but the man was no longer a man. Veiled with glistening wings, Ralph stood before him, shimmering in golden light.

"Who are you?"

"Raphael," he said, and bowed, "Seraph and servant of the Almighty."

"What do you want with me?"

"I bear a message from my Lord concerning your happiness and hers." He nodded toward the door through which Sierra had disappeared.

"I want no message from God. I want an answer to my question. Why does he fail to protect those who love him most? How can they advance His kingdom when they are dead?"

"The heart of man can't comprehend God's reasons. Is your anger against God for their benefit or for yourself? If they truly love him, are they not where they would wish to be? If you truly love them, rejoice for them. Their present state of happiness is more than this earth contains. It is your happiness and hers that concerns God now. It stands in your obedience. He commands you to pray and to be Holy. Take heed lest passion sway your judgement. Satan lies; listen not to his temptations. Listen not to his temptations. Temptations…Temptations…" The angel faded into the moonlit darkness of the bedroom as Josh struggled awake.

He lay staring into the gloom of the ceiling, willing his heart to resume its normal rhythm and hoping that a few moments of solid wakefulness would secure a sound sleep for the rest of the night. "A dream with a football player as an angel." He laughed. "That's really bad casting."

Turning to his side, Josh pounded the pillow. Waiting for sleep to return, he realized that he'd never seen Ralph before the party, and he wondered if Ralph was a football player. The thought occurred to him that Ralph might be a new acquisition, so he decided to make some calls in the morning and check up on him. With that resolution, Josh drifted back to sleep, but the dream returned.

Dawn glimmered through the blinds when his eyes snapped open the third time. He lay watching the room brighten, wondering at the vividness of his vision, and asking himself if Ralph could have been an angel.

"Yeah. Right." He ran a hand through his tousled hair. "Get real McCabe, and get in the shower."

"Flight 231 for Los Angeles now boarding at gate 10." The announcer could be heard even over the buzz of all the conversations in the busy airline terminal.

"That's my flight." Sierra turned to Eleanor. "I have to go now."

With a tremendous effort of self-control, the blond fought back tears. "I know. Give me a hug, brat." She blinked away the moisture flooding her eyes and embraced her cousin. "You write to me and call as often as you can, okay?"

"Yes, I will. Ellie, please go and see Gran frequently. Promise?"

"I promise. Go on now, before you miss your plane." Eleanor firmly turned away and smiled bravely at Josh. "You take care of her."

"Good-by, Eleanor." He shook her hand noncommittally and turned to the other two members of the farewell party. "Ed, thanks for your help with all the luggage and boxes of supplies. It was a pleasure meeting you."

"Don't mention it. I was glad to help." The scholarly seminary student shook Josh's hand, but his eyes were on Eleanor who watched forlornly while her cousin walked away.

"Dr. Cook, I hope to see you again soon," Josh said, and grasped his hand firmly.

"Give your parents my love, son. And remember that I'm always praying for you." Dr. Cook hugged him. "You go now, and catch up with that little gal, before the plane leaves without you."

Four angels hovered over the small group watching the good-byes, knowing that they too must go their separate ways, two of them into the enemy's stronghold.

Several long strides brought Josh to Sierra's side. "What's your hurry? We have plenty of time," he informed her brusquely.

"I hate good-byes," she admitted in a soft voice and wiped at her eye.

"Look on the bright side. They're only temporary."

Surprised at the kindness in his words, she looked at him with new awareness. She couldn't help thinking that Ellie was right. He was very good-looking. Even in comfortable, casual travel clothes, there was a compelling air about him. Clad in tan trousers and matching green plaid shirt, her traveling partner turned more than a few female heads. He smiled down at her, causing her heart to miss a beat and her hands to fumble. She handed the boarding pass to the attendant. "Do you mind if I take the window seat?" she asked, "I enjoy looking out."

"No problem. It doesn't matter to me."

They settled into their seats and buckled up. The roar of the jet engines increased in volume, and soon the plane was zooming down the runway, and they were thrust back in their seats as it lifted off. A little giggle escaped Sierra at the sensation. "I love that part."

Josh smiled at her response. "You don't fly much, do you?"

"No. That is, not since I was little. We flew a lot when I was small. Before my parents were killed, and I went to live with my grandmother."

"Oh, what did your father do for a living?"

"Why, we were missionaries," Sierra said. "I thought you knew. Didn't Dr. Cook tell you?"

"No. He left that part out. How old were you when your parents died? Did they die on the mission field?" He frowned, suddenly feeling compassion for her, and beginning to regret the phone call he'd made to the Jakarta hotel.

"I uh…" She tugged on the neckline of her green sweater. "I was eight years old. We were on home assignment. My parents and I were skiing in Colorado along with Ellie and her parents. There was an avalanche." She swallowed, fighting against the smothering weight. "All four of our parents were killed. Ellie and I went to live with our Grandmother." She ended and looked pensively out the window as the landscape below unfolded.

"But avalanche danger areas are usually clearly marked. It surprises me that they would take such a risk."

She forced herself to turn towards him. "I'd rather not talk about it, Mr. McCabe."

"But," Josh said only to be interrupted by the arrival of the flight hostess.

"Could I get you something to drink?" The stewardess inquired and took their orders. "I'll be right back with that, and your dinners will be ready shortly." She smiled and moved with efficiency down the aisle.

Raphael and Zephon cruised alongside the plane, enjoying the chance to really stretch their wings.

"Your charge seems changed for the better." Zephon observed.

"I visited him in a dream last night," Raphael replied. "It made a strong impression on him."

Josh yawned, shrugged his large shoulders, and sifted in his seat in an effort to get comfortable. He yawned again and frowned, remembering why he was so tired. He couldn't get the dream out of his head, especially after a call to the team office produced a negative answer regarding a new player by the name of Ralph, but he determined anew to exercise willpower over the memory, so he forced it from his thoughts and then shifted restlessly in the confining seat, trying to relax and think of something else.

Sierra looked at the wide shoulders that completely filled the narrow seat. Part of his discomfort was caused by trying to keep his arm on his leg in an effort not to touch her. "You'll be more comfortable with your arm on the armrest." She pointed out and moved her arm to her lap.

"Thanks, I got the impression you didn't want me to touch you, so I was trying to oblige." The angel's image flashed into his mind, and he heard the warning once again.

His comment brought to Sierra's mind the first time he had touched her, making her blush madly.

Josh coughed and looked away. The memory of Sierra in his arms replaced the dream and refused his efforts at resistance.

"You know, Mr. McCabe, you might feel better if you apologized," she said in a gentle rebuke, knowing he was remembering their kiss also.

His green eyes stole slowly over her face to her lips and stopped, then came back to lock with her gaze. He pushed the angel's warning from his mind again. "I can't do that because I'm not sorry. I enjoyed that kiss very much." His voice was husky, leaving her shaken and in no doubt that he would very much like to kiss her again.

"Here we are; dinner is served," a blond flight attendant said as she pulled the service cart to a stop by their seats and handed out their meals.

The hum of jet engines muted the sound of the other diners as Josh and Sierra ate without speaking for awhile.

Distracted by the view, she gazed out the window, watching the landscape. It seemed to float by below. Air travel had delighted her as a small child, and she still found it amazing that such a large ship could fly through the air. Lost in her thoughts, she was unaware that her traveling companion had turned his attention from the food to her.

"So where were your parents serving as missionaries?"

She turned from the window to find his dinner forgotten on his tray as he watched her, his eyes narrowed in contemplation. "In the Sierra Madre mountains of Mexico, among the Cora people. They were Bible translators. They finished a project begun by another couple and had just been reassigned to Irian Jaya."

"You don't say. You're lucky your first assignment was in such a civilized place."

"I don't remember much about it really. Just the joy that my parents took in their work. That's why I want to be a missionary; I want that joy in my life."

He remembered something Eleanor had said. "Is that the only reason? Could there be some guilt involved?"

She sat up straighter. "I resent that question, Mr. McCabe. You have no right to question my motives. Isn't the joy of serving God enough reason?"

He frowned and looked away. "You're not much like your cousin, are you?"

Startled by his sudden change of subject, she paused before answering, and asked herself what had made him change the subject. The thought that it was because he had no joy in his life made her heart hurt for him, and she cautioned herself to be careful lest he sneak past her defenses. Realizing he was waiting for an answer, she replied. "No, but then we're only cousins. Our fathers were very different, and they were brothers. My father's only goal in life was to serve God and be a good husband and father. Ellie's dad was a lawyer. They didn't go to church much. I think her parents quarreled a lot. They were very wealthy and bought Ellie everything she wanted. It's hard to deny Eleanor when she has her heart set on something; not only is she beautiful, but she's very persuasive. Add to that an enthusiastic, extroverted personality, and she seems to have everything, except the most important thing."

Josh's comment had been more of an observation than a question, and he was surprised that she answered. The information about Ellie was interesting, and just watching her expressive face as she spoke fascinated him. "Oh, what's that?"

"She isn't saved," Sierra answered sadly, "but that may change in the near future. I think God is in the process of answering that prayer."

"You love her very much, don't you?"

"Yes, she's really more like my sister than my cousin. Do you have any brothers or sisters?"

Darkness descended over his face. "Not any more." He folded his arms and closed his eyes. "Thanks for the conversation, but I need a nap."

Chapter 7

"Good morning ladies and gentlemen." The pilot's voice crackled from the speaker.

It woke Sierra. She yawned, stretched, and glanced around her in hazy recognition of her surroundings while listening to the pilot.

"We're flying at ten thousand feet and making very good time. We should be arriving in Jakarta in approximately two hours. If you'll direct your attention to the scenery below, you'll see we have an extraordinarily clear view of the islands of Indonesia. The country of Indonesia is made up of over thirteen thousand islands that are actually part of the Malay Archipelago. The official language for the nation is Indonesian, which is based on Malay, but there are actually hundreds of languages spoken by the natives. Some native tribes are so isolated they have had no contact with the modern world. I hope you'll enjoy your stay in the exotic, beautiful, and mysterious country of Indonesia."

"Very knowledgeable, isn't he?" Sierra observed, aware that her traveling companion had awakened.

"Yes, he is," Josh replied, but in truth he'd barely heard the pilot because his mind was far away, planning Sierra's abrupt departure from Irian Jaya before she became its next victim. He wondered how she would react to his little surprise, and a cynical little smile turned up one corner of his mouth.

In response to a shrill whistle from Josh, a yellow taxi with a flashing dome light screeched to a halt by the curb outside the airport where Josh and Sierra stood near their pile of luggage. The driver, a tall slender man of regal bearing, came to stand before them and bowed with the palm of his right hand to his forehead.

"Peace be unto you. My name is Prince Patel. May I be of assistance?" He smiled, and it lit his eyes, reaching out to embrace them like welcome friends. His smile was impossible to resist.

Sierra and Josh introduced themselves, and Josh gave the name of their hotel, while helping load the luggage.

Reluctant to sit down again after the long flight, Sierra watched the men, curious about the contrasts in the driver. He had the name of an East Indian, and he wore a turban, but he dressed in Western clothing, light cotton slacks and a long sleeved shirt. Most intriguing of all, a prayer rug sat in the front passenger seat, and he had greeted them in the traditional manner of a devout Muslim, but in American accented English. That accent never failed during the men's conversation.

Raphael and Zephon watched also, along with their new friend, Nadu. They hovered above the group, sharing information about enemy movement and guarding against threats.

"There, last bag," Prince said, and slammed the trunk. "Since this is your first time in Jakarta, Miss Evans, would you like to see a few sights on the way to your hotel?" He opened the cab door for her.

"Yes. That would be lovely. Thank you," she replied and climbed in.

Without a word, Josh nodded his head at the driver and took a seat beside her, but he didn't look very happy.

Prince smiled at them in the rearview mirror, flipped on his meter, and sped down the airport causeway like an arrow shot from a bow. Darting around slower vehicles and the many mopeds that filled the streets, he seemed oblivious to the blaring horns and angry shouts that followed their progress towards the center of Jakarta, hardly slowing until they approached a large building with a lush green lawn and tall trees.

He waved toward the building and looked in the mirror at Josh and Sierra. "This is the Central Museum, known as the Gedung Gajah or 'Elephant Building' because of the unusual lawn ornament." He nodded toward a bigger than life size stone elephant on the lawn.

"Wow," Sierra breathed. "He looks so real, as if waiting for a Rajah to climb onto his back and ride off to his palace."

"If you have time, Miss Evans," Prince said, "I recommend that you visit the museum; it contains an extensive collection of artifacts and relics that date back to the Stone Age, including bronzes and ceramics from the Han, Tang, and Ming Dynasties."

"Oh, that sounds fascinating. I'd love to see it," Sierra replied, then looked at Josh. "Maybe I'll have time tomorrow morning."

"No." He shook his head. "Our itinerary is full."

She looked back at Prince. "I'll make a point to schedule some time for it on my next visit to Jakarta."

He smiled and motioned toward the front of the vehicle. "Just ahead is one of my favorite artistic structures in Jakarta."

An enormous fountain came into view. At its center, a horse drawn chariot, ridden by two men, raced through torrents of water. The attention to detail in every rippling muscle of man and beast made the artwork come to life.

Prince slowed the taxi slightly, and veered closer. "Arjuna, the archer, and Krishna, god of transcendental self." The cab careened back into heavy traffic while Prince continued. "Keep watching the sky in front of us and you'll see the National Monument, better known as Monas."

A couple of minutes later, Sierra spotted it. Against the Equatorial blue sky, a white marble obelisk topped by a flame of pure gold reached toward heaven. When Prince pulled the cab into the drive that circled it, Sierra had to roll the cab window down in order to see the whole structure. "It's hundreds of feet tall," she said, craning her neck to see the top.

"Over four hundred feet," Prince said, " and the flame is coated with over seventy pounds of gold." He slowed the taxi almost coming to a complete stop. "To the people of Jakarta, it is the symbol of freedom. But to those that know Him, there is a greater symbol," he whispered the last sentence, and then met Sierra's eyes in the mirror and smiled. "When you have time, take the elevator to the top for a view of the city and the sea. It would only take a moment." At a nod from Josh, Prince pulled over.

When Sierra opened her door, she heard the cry of a muezzin calling the faithful to prayer. She was not surprised when Prince turned off the meter, spread his rug on the grass and knelt to pray. He prayed in Arabic, and Sierra listened to the guttural eruptions and long flowing vowels as she walked toward the obelisk with Josh. The view from the top was even more spectacular than Prince had claimed, but she couldn't wait to gain the ground once more. The words of Prince's prayer kept repeating in her head. Arabic wasn't one of her strongest languages, but she had distinctly heard Prince praising the name of Issa, the Arabic name for Jesus, and she wanted to ask him about it. Once on the ground level, Sierra and Josh headed toward the cab in time to see their driver finish his prayers and stand. He turned to face them and the sun illuminated his face—peace, intense and blissful, radiated from it in a glow brighter than the golden flame behind them.

"He loves God," she whispered.

"Poor fool," Josh replied.

"How dare you!" Sierra's eyes burned with anger. "That's a despicable thing to say," she hissed and then fell silent when they reached the cab.

Prince's gaze flew from Sierra's face to Josh, but he only motioned to the cab. "Shall we continue the tour?"

"I think that's enough," Josh said.

The cab careened back into heavy traffic while Prince continued. "If you like Colonial architecture, especially homes, be sure and visit the Menteng Residential area, and if you like shopping for deals, try the Jalan Surabaya; that's our local flea market. Ah, here we are. Safe and sound at your hotel." He pulled the cab to an abrupt halt under the hotel canopy and opened the door for Sierra.

The street noise assaulted her ears when Sierra stepped from the cab, effectively blocking out the conversation between Josh and Prince. Sierra waved as the cab pulled away. "What a charming man," she said.

"In his business, it pays to be charming," he replied and followed her into the hotel.

The cacophony of the streets of Jakarta receded into welcome quiet when they entered the hotel's wide doors. Wine red carpet muffled their footsteps as they walked through the walnut paneled lobby to the desk. Josh immediately gave the clerk their names.

Sierra pressed her lips together, refusing to give in to the surge of irritation at his silent treatment. He'd hardly spoken a word to her since she'd rebuked him. She turned away, surveying the rattan furniture nestled amongst tropical plants in the spacious lobby, but she swung around, her eyes widening when she heard the clerk's reply to Josh.

"I'm sorry sir, but there seems to be a mistake. There's only one room reserved for a Mr. Joshua McCabe and Miss Sierra Evans."

"We'll need an additional room," Sierra insisted.

"I'm afraid that won't be possible miss. The hotel is full."

"Would you call and find us accommodations at another hotel please," Josh said calmly, as if in an effort not to lose his temper, but he forced back a grin.

"I'll try sir, but Jakarta has suffered a great influx of people, and our housing construction has not caught up to the demand." The desk clerk rushed to explain before turning to his telephone.

Zephon and Raphael exchanged glances. "The enemy failed in his frontal attacks, so now he tries sabotage," he said.

"He may plan a frontal attack for later if the room situation can't be resolved," Zephon observed.

Sierra put a hand to the lace on her collar and swallowed. "Oh, but there must be another room somewhere."

"You heard what he said," Josh turned to face her. "And you saw the crowds on the way from the airport. This city is jam-packed with people. It has been for years. Some things never change." Contrary to the seriousness of the situation, a little smile turned up one corner of his mouth.

Sierra saw his amusement, and little arrows of alarm darted through her. "But we can't share a room." Panicked by the vivid picture her mind painted, she sent a silent but fervent prayer heavenward, asking God to work out the room situation, but her pulse refused to subside, especially when the clerk turned back to them.

The sad look on the clerk's face told the story even before he spoke. "I'm sorry sir; every hotel in the city is full."

"Thank you for your trouble. We'll take our room key now." Josh wiped the smile of success from his face before he turned to Sierra.

"This is simply out of the question," she hissed. "I refuse to share a room with you. I'd rather sleep in the lobby."

In a steely quiet voice that brooked no disagreement, Josh recited their itinerary. "Early tomorrow afternoon our plane leaves for Sentani, and from there a missionary pilot will fly us to the mission station at Kokonau. From there we travel by foot for approximately seven hours into the foothills of Jaya Peak, where the village is located. It's a very long and exhausting trip. The heat is intense, and the bugs are worse. You'll need to be well rested before we leave tomorrow. I refuse to deposit a sick female on my parent's doorstep." The elevator door closed as he finished, and he released her arm that he had taken, fully expecting an argument.

He did not have long to wait. Sierra had tried in vain to control her mounting ire. "I'm never sick, and I resent being referred to like I'm the morning newspaper. And I'll thank you not to manhandle me in public or any other place, Mr. McCabe." Her turquoise eyes darkened as fire flashed from them, and her cheeks flushed pale rose in anger, rivaling the color of her blouse. To her dismay, Josh started to smile, and then he chuckled. Too amazed by his reaction to be conscious of her actions, she followed him into the room. When he stopped abruptly and turned to face her, Sierra found herself standing very close to Josh. She stared in fascination at the warm twinkle in his dark green eyes.

"I was beginning to wonder if all that red hair was just for show." His hand brushed the hair back from her cheek where a silken wave had fallen forward.

The gentle touch of his hand stopped her breath in her throat and caused her heartbeat to accelerate madly. She forced herself to breathe and with great determination backed away from him.

At her reaction, the smile left his face, and his eyes hardened. Ignoring her instincts warning her to proceed with caution, Sierra blurted, "I'll thank you to keep your hands to yourself, Mr. McCabe."

In a move so fast she had no time to flee, he pulled her to within inches of his body. "My name is Josh. Say it," he demanded.

Raphael and Zephon drew their swords the moment they entered the hotel room, expecting to encounter demon activity. When Josh pulled Sierra close, Zephon raised her flashing sword, ready to drive the demons away. "Where are they? I don't see them." She darted in circles around the couple, but saw nothing.

"There are no demons, only the desires within them," Raphael said, and nodded toward the couple. He remained vigilant for interference from the foe, but he made no move toward his charge.

"Do something." Zephon looked from Raphael to Josh.

Raphael shook his head. "The humans have free will. They must decide to obey God because they love him, or to follow the inclinations of their flesh. What good is love unless it is freely given? We must not interfere."

Zephon looked at Sierra, and gripped her sword harder, willing her charge to resist. "But it isn't free will. He's forcing her!"

"Isn't it?" Raphael nodded toward the couple.

Sierra pressed both hands against Josh's chest, intending to push away, then stopped. Incredibly aware of the feel of his hard muscles under her hands where they rested on his chest, to her horror Sierra found herself wanting to move her hands in exploration. She couldn't believe that she was being seduced by the man who was supposed to be protecting her, and her mind cried out to God for help. A surge of strength and will power that she knew could only have come from her father in heaven filled her with resolve. She pushed free of his grasp. "Mr. McCabe, I'm very disappointed to find that the man whom Dr. Cook loves like a son could behave in such an ungentlemanly way."

"Praise God!" Zephon shouted and heaved a sigh of relief.

Sierra's statement put the brakes on Josh's run-away desire more effectively than any words she could have said, and he had the grace to look ashamed of himself. His plan was not coming together the way he had envisioned.

"Really, Mr. McCabe, I'm willing to forgive your behavior at Ellie's party because you were obviously not yourself. But I would appreciate it if you would not continue with these unwelcome advances."

"Unwelcome advances?" He laughed, and his eyes turned frosty as snow coated evergreens. "The beginning of our kiss at the party might have been unwelcome, but by the end you were kissing me back."

"That's absurd," she protested, licking her lips and nervously locking white teeth on her bottom lip. "I didn't even know you. I don't kiss strange men."

Like a cloud obscuring the sun from an evergreen glen, his eyes darkened as they fastened on her teeth reddened lip. His intent was clear even before he spoke, "I can prove you kissed me back." He stepped forward as if to make good his threat.

She sidestepped to evade him and gasped at her first full view of the room. "Oh no!"

Josh pivoted in an automatic response to her gasp.

The source of her dismay sat threateningly in the middle of the room. Its large square solitary bulk screamed danger as surely as if it had been decorated with a skull and crossbones.

"You'll have to sleep outside the door." Sierra spoke without thought and realized her error when she felt her antagonist bristle.

"And if I refuse?"

"I might have known you wouldn't be a gentleman about this. As you demonstrated quite succinctly the first time I laid eyes on you."

He chuckled wickedly. "Are you trying to remind me of what I was about to do before you discovered there was only one bed in this room?" He laughed even more when he saw the anger flash in her eyes and a lovely blush suffuse her cheeks once again, but his laughter contained an element of irony because he realized he couldn't follow through with his plan to seduce her, even though he had hoped she would leave the mission field forever, believing herself a fallen woman.

But Sierra didn't recognize his change of heart; she only heard the laughter, and her temper raged—she closed her eyes, clenched her fists, and struggled for control. She had never been so angry in her life, and she wanted to hit him more than she'd ever wanted to hit anyone. She forced herself to pray, crying out for help until her anger subsided. "Very well," she replied, and looked at him, measurably calmer. "Since you refuse, I'll sleep outside the door."

"Don't be an idiot," he exclaimed in exasperation and began unbuttoning his shirt.

Fascinated, but equally horrified by the brown skin being exposed by his actions, she forced her gaze to his face. "What are you doing?"

"I'm taking a shower. A very cold shower." With bag in hand, he entered the bathroom and firmly closed the door, only to snap it open. "And don't leave. You win. After I bring you back from the restaurant, I'll sleep somewhere else."

"But, I…" Sierra started to protest, but the door closed. "What restaurant?" she said to the closed door. "I didn't say I'd go to a restaurant with you. I've never met anyone in my life that had so much nerve." Clamping a lid on her temper, she flung her suitcase on the monstrous bed and rummaged through the bag for a change of clothing, all the while knowing she should pray, but unable to formulate the words.

Chapter 8

When they walked into the restaurant later, a darkly handsome man came forward to meet them. "Josh, my good friend. It's good to see you." The smiling man clasped Josh's hand, his black eyes lit with joy in his sculptured bronze face. "It's been a long time since I last saw you, my friend. I see the Lord's blessed you with the company of a beautiful woman. Is she your nyonya?"

"Sierra Evans, this is Jonti Kapur. Jon and I grew up together. My parents worked among his people for eighteen years, translating the Bible into their language and starting a church. Sierra is a linguist, Jon. She's going to help my parents in their new assignment."

"I'm so glad to meet you Mr. Kapur," she said, and extended her hand with a radiant smile. "I couldn't help but notice your reference to the Lord. Are you a Christian?"

His well-groomed wavy hair reflected the soft lighting of the restaurant. He bowed over her hand. "Please, call me Jon. And yes, I'm a Christian. My good friend Josh led me to the Lord many years ago when we were both children. Miss Evans, it's with great pleasure that I welcome you to my restaurant."

Zephon lifted her dark brows and looked at Raphael. "Your charge has brought someone to the Lord?"

He nodded. "More than one."

A new respect warmed the small angel's attitude toward Josh.

"Josh, my friend. The Lord is smiling on you tonight, your favorite table is available. Please follow me." Jonti nodded at Sierra and led them through the elegantly decorated restaurant.

With casual ease Josh held Sierra's chair for her at the secluded table. Well-placed plants created a gentle screen from the other diners.

"I hope you will enjoy your dinner." Jon handed them menus and bowed. "Please order anything your heart desires. After all, it's on the house."

The two men chuckled, and Sierra wondered what was so funny.

"Why don't you join us," Josh said. "It'll be good to catch up on what's happening in your life."

"Thank you for your kind invitation my friend, but I would leave you now to enjoy the evening with your lady. I request however, if time allows, that you both join me for brunch tomorrow."

"That would be great, Jon," Josh said. "I'll do that, but I can't speak for Sierra." He looked at her with narrowing eyes, and the ready anger flared up to challenge her.

She realized that he didn't want her to accept Jon's invitation. With a lift of her chin, she flashed a smile at Jon. "I'd love to come."

"Very good. Konahario until then my friends." With a graceful bow, he turned and melted into the dimly lit restaurant.

"What a wonderful man," Sierra observed as she opened her menu. "He has such beautiful manners."

The slight inflection on the pronoun might have escaped another's ears, but not Josh's. "Meaning that I don't? Do you polish your halo every morning Sierra? You proved you're not perfect when you yelled at me in the hotel room."

"I do not yell." She corrected him, her spine stiffening, but she realized her voice had risen, and she slumped. "Please stop baiting me. Fighting will ruin the evening. This is a beautiful restaurant." She looked around with admiration at the well-appointed tables, placed without crowding in the blue and gold room. A white grand piano, under a sparkling chandelier, graced the center of the room, and a Strauss waltz danced from the fingertips of the pianist. She resisted the temptation to sway to its rhythm.

"Jon has done very well for himself for a boy from the Irian jungle."

"Did I hear him correctly? He owns this restaurant?" She frowned at the menu.

"Half owner, actually," he answered, while observing her look of indecision over the food. "If you like seafood and curry, try the shrimp. It's the best I've ever tasted."

"Thank you, I think I will." She folded her menu, placing it at the table's edge. "It must be quite a story how your friend came from the jungle to this."

"It is." Josh placed their orders and then continued. "Right from the start, Jonti was special. His father taught us their language and helped my parents began translation work. My mother began teaching the children of the village. Jon soaked everything up like a sponge and wanted more. At the age of twelve, I was shipped off to the missionary kids' academy in the Philippines. My parents saw the potential in Jon and arranged for him to attend also. He graduated with honors and won a scholarship to Oxford. He could have been anything he wanted, but from the first time he set foot in a first class restaurant, this was his heart's desire."

"What a wonderful story. Jon loves the Lord very much, doesn't he?" She looked into his eyes in search of a clue to his own relationship with God, but he averted his eyes from her penetrating gaze.

"Yes." After the clipped reply he fell silent, a muscle flexing repeatedly in his jaw. After their argument in the hotel room, he feared that he couldn't convince Sierra to give up her obsession to go off into the jungle where her life was in danger, and that revelation brought him to the conclusion that he needed to stay away from her. He couldn't. Visions of the trouble that she could encounter left on her own in a strange, and crime-ridden, city demanded that he bring her with him. He questioned his decision to bring her to the restaurant because the romantic setting undermined his resolve to harden his emotions against her.

Sierra hadn't noticed the battle within Josh. She continued in her observations about Jonti. "I thought so. He has a special radiance in his eyes. 'Delight yourself in the Lord and he will give you the desire of your heart,'" she quoted with a little smile.

"And what is the desire of your heart Sierra?" he asked. The gentle smile on her face sent a wave crashing through him against his will; it surged against the wall around his heart, ripping at its foundation.

"Only to serve God the best that I can with the gifts and abilities he has given me. Isn't that what every true Christian wants?" In response to her question, a shadow passed over his face, and a fleeting look of pain reminded her of the sorrow she had glimpsed before.

He raised his water goblet and watched the crystal sparkle in the light, wondering if he should tell her the whole gruesome story.

The arrival of their dinner saved him from a response. Their food was presented in a delightful arrangement that displayed the artistry of the chef. The aromas teased Sierra's senses making her mouth water in anticipation. She thanked the waiter and bowed her head waiting for Josh to ask God's blessing on the food. A prolonged silence greeted her action. She looked up to find him staring at her.

"If you're waiting for me to pray, you'll have a long wait." He picked up his eating utensils and applied them to his food.

Pain pierced her heart when she realized just how estranged he was from the Lord. *Father in heaven; please help Josh to come back to you. Heal his pain, and restore him to your fellowship. For your glory Father. In Jesus' name, amen.* Sierra kept her head bowed as she began eating, not wanting Josh to see the tears that brightened her eyes.

"Is your food good?" he asked after an extended silence.

She blinked to clear away the telltale moisture and looked up at him. "Yes, it's very good. I love these tiny green beans. They almost melt in your mouth."

"Is it too hot for you? Your eyes are watering."

"Oh, uh, it's a little hotter than I'm used to." She hedged and reached for her water glass. Fearful that he might suspect the real reason for her tears, she tried to distract him. "What time is our plane leaving tomorrow?"

"Not until early afternoon, so we'll have plenty of time to have brunch with Jon. I'm assuming you're an early riser." He commented with a lifted brow.

She smiled, but it didn't reach her eyes. "Yes. But I might get hit with jet lag." She set her fork down. "That was delicious. I'm so stuffed. I don't think I can eat another bite."

"Don't you want dessert? They have a superb fudge cake."

"Oh," she groaned. "Don't tempt me." With a frowning squint, she tilted her head to the side. "How did you know fudge cake is my favorite dessert?"

He lifted his eyebrows and grinned, looking like a mischievous boy, and Sierra felt the warmth of his eyes suffuse her very being. They reminded her of the forest against a midsummer blue sky, mysterious deep green.

"I read your mind," he stated with a challenge in his tone.

Sierra hoped that he hadn't. She was acutely aware that her thoughts at the moment were treading on very dangerous ground.

He laughed at her worried expression. "Truthfully, I saw the box of candy you have stashed in your suitcase."

She grinned in relief. "That was a going away present from Ellie. She knows I have a weakness for See's candy."

"Trust Ellie to cater to indulgences of the flesh. Speaking of which, if you don't want dessert, how about coffee?"

"That sounds wonderful. I need something to help me digest all that food."

He ordered their coffee and turned his attention back to her, noticing her fascination with the variety of exotically dressed diners.

"This is the most exciting time in all of history to be alive," she said with a thrill in her voice. "I mean, look at us, sitting here in a restaurant in Indonesia, and it only took us hours to get here. Less than a hundred years ago, it took missionaries months of arduous travel to reach the people God sent them to. And travel is not the only thing that's improved tremendously; communication is so much better now. We have radio stations that reach people where the gospel has not been allowed to go. There are television and videos that are used in new and innovative ways. And computers, of course, have made Bible translation so much easier and efficient than it was even twenty years ago. I thank God that he has allowed me to live in a time when we're coming so close to fulfilling the Great Commission."

Her statement was made with such profound gratitude and obvious love that Josh felt a wave of something like homesickness sweep over him. "When you talk like that you remind me very much of—" He fell silent, and a dark shadow slipped over his face.

His voice sounded so unhappy, it almost brought tears to her eyes again. "Who do I remind you of?"

"It doesn't matter. They're gone now." He looked away to the dance floor where satiated diners moved with grace to a contemporary waltz. "Dance with me, Sierra." He regretted the invitation the moment that it left his mouth, but something within him refused to retract it.

Zephon tensed, and her hand went to her sword as she scanned the area for the enemy.

Raphael shook his head. "They are not here. Jonti's guardian, Ithuriel, presents a formidable barrier to their activity in this establishment."

Say no, Sierra. Zephon urged silently.

To say no would have been the wiser choice, but her heart hurt for him, and she silenced her brain's objections, stood, and moved into his arms as if under a spell. The spell deepened and reality receded.

Desire like a stalking lion ran rampant through Josh as he held her body close to his. The silk of her hair brushed his hand at her waist, making him want to bury his hands in its luxuriant length and kiss her until she was breathless.

"Do you know you are the most beautiful woman I've ever seen."

The huskiness of his voice stopped the beating of her heart as the last note of the music stopped the dancers.

She pushed away from him. "Did you really think I would fall for that line, Mr. McCabe? Women like Ellie are beautiful, not redheads with freckles." With great effort she forced her legs to move and collected her purse from their table. "I'd like to return to the hotel now."

"Coward. You can't run away from what just happened between us."

Her head tilted with defiance. "Nothing just happened."

"And now you've added lying to cowardice," he accused.

"Mr. McCabe, are you going to escort me back to the hotel, or do I go by myself," she demanded.

At her formal use of his name, his jaw tightened, and he looked as if he would like to throttle her. Visibly controlling his temper, he flipped several bills on the table and escorted her from the restaurant.

Chapter 9

The sun played peek-a-boo behind whipped cream clouds in a deep blue sky when they stepped from the hotel the next morning. Summoning a taxi to carry them to brunch with Jonti, Josh placed two fingers in his mouth and whistled shrilly. Rewarding his effort, a yellow cab pulled up to the curb, and Prince smiled at them.

Josh gave the address to the friendly driver, and Sierra gave him a warm greeting, then stifled a scream and held on when the cab pulled into traffic with no regard for oncoming cars. Zigzagging at breakneck speed, Prince made his way across town, paying little attention to traffic lights and stop signs.

Raphael and Zephon flew along outside the cab, watching for any activity from the enemy. The potential hazards from the traffic and the cabbie's driving style raised their senses to high alert.

Sierra shifted a wide-eyed gaze to find Josh smiling, apparently enjoying himself immensely.

She wondered where he had spent the night. After returning with her to the hotel after their dinner, Josh grabbed his suitcase, warned her to lock the door and not leave the room, and departed. He called shortly after daybreak and asked her to meet him in the lounge in two hours in order to leave for their scheduled brunch with Jonti. Wherever he'd stayed, he looked well rested in gray slacks and pinstriped shirt.

She asked in wonder. "Do all the Jakarta taxi drivers operate their vehicles this way?"

"No, most of them go faster. I think Prince needs a tune-up on this baby. Relax, you'd be amazed at how few accidents they have."

"I'm sure—" She began, only to end with a small shriek. Prince slammed on his brakes and took a corner at breakneck speed, tires squealing all the way. The cab's momentum sent Sierra flying across the seat to find herself being held to Josh's broad chest by two hard muscled arms. Dark turquoise eyes locked with forest green, and Sierra's breath hung suspended. Her heart fluttered like a trapped bird.

Zephon started to enter the cab, but Raphael raised his hand. "You'll find no enemy there," he said. She obeyed, but kept a watchful eye on her charge.

Josh gazed at the freckles on Sierra's nose while his hand stroked the silken tresses that wrapped around them both in charming disarray. His mind told him to release her, but his arms refused to obey. He felt the wild beating of her heart and spoke gently. "You see, there are unexpected pleasures that await us in these madcap taxi rides."

With both hands she pushed against the solid wall of his chest, and to her surprise, he released her without hesitation.

A wry smile turned up one corner of his mouth while he stared at her face. "Don't ever try to earn a living playing poker. You'd starve. Your face shows exactly what you're thinking. For instance, just now I saw fear and desire while I held you in my arms, then surprise and disappointment when I released you."

"Don't flatter yourself, Mr. McCabe." Sierra felt the heat in her cheeks and looked away, rearranging the skirt of her island print dress. "Fear, I'll grant you because you've proved to be no gentleman and surprise for the same reason, but the other two are the product of your own imagination."

"What's the matter? Can't you even say the word desire Sierra? Admit that you wanted me to kiss you, and you were disappointed when I didn't."

"I'm not going to admit anything of the kind." She looked around in bewilderment as they left Jakarta behind and traveled toward some hills to the northwest. "Where on earth are we going? Where does Jonti live?"

"It's not much farther now." Slashing her with his eyes, he leaned back and folded his arms across his chest.

Within moments Prince turned onto a side road, which wound around, up and over a hill, before turning one last curve and bringing them into a tiny tree dotted village on a small plateau.

"Oh, how beautiful," she whispered.

The cottages of the village, painted in varying shades of rose, adorned the verdant hillside and looked out over a seemingly endless expanse of the Java Sea.

Josh paid Prince and included a handsome tip with the promise of another if the driver would return for them in three hours. Sierra stood entranced only half listening to their conversation.

"Jon will be glad you like his village. Come on. His home is the third one on the right."

The door opened before they reached it, and Jonti stood smiling on the threshold. "Konahario and welcome. Please come in. I have a surprise for you my friend."

His guardian, Ithuriel, stood by Jonti's side, and raised a hand in greeting to Raphael and Zephon. Behind Jonti, another angel hovered, and Zephon recognized Mishiel, a smaller guardian like herself.

Josh and Sierra entered a comfortable but modest living room, decorated in masculine tones softened by bright throw pillows. A young woman stood to greet them. In a face of exquisite bone structure, winged brows set off her wide almond shaped eyes, and her skin was the most flawless Sierra had ever seen. Her black silk pants and top added an illusion of height, but she barely reached five feet.

"Kimi," Josh exclaimed, and his expression relaxed into a look of true pleasure. "It's wonderful to see you. Have you come to help Jon with his project for awhile?"

A smile of pure love lit Kimi's face. She embraced Josh with enthusiasm.

Jonti laughed at the happy reunion and placed a possessive arm around the Kimi's shoulders. "Josh, my friend. Kimi hasn't come to help for awhile. She is here permanently. She is my nyonya."

"Leave it to you to marry the prettiest girl in the village while my back is turned." Josh hugged his friend and pounded him heartily on the back. "When did this happen? Why wasn't I invited to the wedding?"

"We were married a little over a year ago," Jonti explained, and his expression saddened. "We sent word to your parents, but they were unable to get in touch with you. We missed the blessing of your presence at our wedding, my friend, but I understand you were still grieving."

Sierra smiled, then frowned and wondered about the details of Josh's grief.

Josh turned to include her. "Sierra Evans, this is Kimi Kapur, the girl who stole my heart when I was seven years old and now has broken it by marrying my best friend." He teased, smiling with boyish charm.

She extended her hand and greeted Jonti's wife. "It's a pleasure to meet you Kimi. I hope we can become good friends."

"The pleasure is mine, and I would like that very...Oh!" Her response was cut short by a baby's cry. "Please excuse me. I must see to my son." She released Sierra's hand and turned to disappear down the hallway.

"More surprises Jon?" Josh said. "I see congratulations are due you twice over. A son, you lucky guy. You didn't waste any time, did you?" He thumped Jonti's shoulder, shaking his head with a grin.

Jonti accepted the compliments with a smile of pride and turned when Kimi re-entered the room, a small bundle cradled in her arms.

"Oh, how precious," Sierra whispered. The newborn waved tiny clenched fists and opened wide his smoky blue eyes. "May I hold him?"

Kimi smiled and nodded and with care placed the little one in Sierra's arms.

Sierra bent her head over the baby, and her fingers gently touched the baby's cheek. "He's so beautiful. His skin looks and feels just like velvet."

Tightness grew in Josh's chest as he watched her cuddle the baby, and he took a step back, crossed his arms, and tried to look away, but her face, so filled with happiness, held him captive. He swallowed, fighting a tidal wave of emotion, and reminded himself that he wasn't going to get involved.

"My friend, I hope you do not mind," Jonti said. "We have named our son Joshua James Kapur."

Glad of the reprieve, Josh turned to his friend. "I'm deeply honored Jon, and I know my father will be also that you've named your son after us."

The wonderful smell of food, redolent with sweet exotic spices, filled the room as a door opened. A tiny wizened lady with white hair appeared in the doorway. Behind her stood a fifth angel, Merion, who waved to Raphael and Zephon.

"Sayo," Josh cried and swept the diminutive grandmother into a fierce bear hug.

Cackling with glee, she returned his embrace and then scolded him. "Es! That's enough, Tuan Josh. Let me look at you." Pushing away, she studied his face for long moments and then smiled. "Der, der, it is good. You are looking very well. But enough of this, introduce me to your nyonya," she demanded, straightened her blue dress, and turned to Sierra, scanning her from head to toe and nodding.

"Sayo Kapur, Grandmother of my heart, this is Sierra Evans. Sierra is on her way to work with my parents. They're having trouble with the new language they're learning, and she's going to help. She's very gifted in linguistics," Josh added.

Blushing at the unexpected praise, Sierra glanced at Josh in astonishment. She reached out to take the age worn hand of the old woman.

Black eyes gazed deeply into dark turquoise as the old grandmother clasped the young woman's hand in both of hers. Sayo's head tilted from side to side, and a look of puzzlement clouded her face. "I feel as if I know you. And yet, how can this be? Somewhere in my memory there is such a one as you, with hair like fire and eyes as blue as the sky. Why can I not remember? Es! It is enough. Come, our breakfast waits for us."

"Grandmother and Kimi have prepared a feast for us," Jon proclaimed as they followed Sayo into a bright and cheery kitchen.

In an octagonal breakfast nook that looked out on the view, a large round table was set with blue willow china and covered with a vast assortment of fruits and breads. A mouth-watering aroma emanated from a fondue in the center of the table where tiny sausages floated in a bubbling sauce.

Sayo lifted the lids from several warming pans to display golden scrambled eggs, steaming with moisture, pancakes, exuding the essence of butter, and hash browns, standing high in crispy mounds. "Now if my grandson would be so kind as to ask our Lord's blessing on our meal, we may eat."

Sayo reached out to take the hand of Kimi on her right and Jonti on her left, clearly indicating that she wanted them all to be united in prayer, and bowed her head in reverence. Sierra gave her right hand to Jonti as she held the baby cradled in her left arm.

Josh took Kimi's hand and then discovered there was only one way to make the circle unbroken. He realized Jonti and his family had moved to leave him standing by Sierra, but he found himself wishing they hadn't. He had refused to look at her since she took the baby in her arms, and a pounding from Jimbo sounded better than touching her at the moment. Recognizing that he had no choice, but keeping a distance between their bodies, he placed his arm around Sierra's shoulders.

Raphael and Zephon had relaxed their vigilance, feeling secure in the company of other angels, but when Josh touched Sierra, Zephon came to full attention.

Ithuriel laid a hand on her shoulder in reassurance. "The foe would not dare to enter the presence of five angels in the midst of those who pray frequently and fervently." He nodded to every adult in the room but Josh.

Zephon felt the truth of his words when Jonti begin to pray and power surged through her.

Jonti praised God for the beautiful day and the wonderful food that had been prepared with love. He added an entreaty for God to protect Josh and Sierra while they traveled to the village where James and Elizabeth McCabe worked.

Josh heard him as though he spoke through a long tunnel. He refused to take part in the prayer and forced his mind to move toward other things—food, football, the weather—anything but the communication in progress in the room and the woman standing next to him. Josh became aware that the prayer had ended, and he jerked his arm from Sierra.

Kimi reached for her son. "If you please, we will put Baby Joshua in his safety seat, then we may all enjoy our breakfast."

"Of course." With care Sierra handed over the newborn, and then sat down. "The food looks and smells so wonderful."

"Here, try this," Jonti said, passing the fondue to Sierra. "It tastes even better than it smells."

She spooned several tiny sausages in a steaming sauce onto her plate and passed the fondue before taking a bite. "Scrumptious. The flavor is like nothing I've ever tasted. It's superb."

Grandmother Sayo beamed, and said, "Enjoy, enjoy," then she lapsed into silence, contemplating the foreign woman's hair and eyes. Intense concentration showed on her face, marked by narrowed eyes and pursed lips.

Between bites Sierra turned to Jonti. "Josh tells me you grew up together in Irian Jaya. How old were you Jonti when Josh and his parents came to your village?" Sierra took another bite and glanced up to find Josh staring at her. The look on his face sent her heart skipping until she realized she had inadvertently used his first name. Her color rose, and she turned away.

"I was seven years old, as was Josh. This tuan boy, with eyes like the jungle, wanted to become a great hunter." Jonti's dark eyes sparkled. "I was, of course, already greatly skilled and condescended to share my immense knowledge with him." He laughed at the memory of his little boy bravado. "Much to my dismay, my friend soon surpassed me in skills and bravery."

Pleased by his friend's praise, Josh smiled. "If I surpassed you, it was only by chance, or perhaps because I had such an excellent teacher. You took this poor tuan kid and helped him adjust to a totally different culture."

"My friend, anything I did for you was as nothing compared to the gift your family has given to my people. You taught us who God really is. My people were awakened from a sleep that ends in death and given new life as surely as the dawn brings light to the day."

A startled gasp followed Jonti's last words, and everyone turned to find Sayo staring at Sierra; a physical manifestation of every angel in the room wouldn't have widened Sayo's eyes more. Dismay gave way to pure unadulterated joy until she seemed ready to burst with it. "You are the one! Praise God, let it be so," she whispered with reverence and lifted her hands toward heaven.

"What Grandmother?" Jonti reached out to her, alarmed by her intense excitement.

She grasped his hand and squeezed it in reassurance. "I am all right Grandson. I have remembered. It was your words Jonti that brought the legend back to my mind. It is a very old story, told to me by my grandmother many long years ago. My grandmother was not of our tribe, the Dani. The Dani fought with my grandmother's people, the Kai. They were fierce enemies for many years until Tuan Josh's parents brought the love of God to the Dani village. My grandmother was captured as a young girl. She would have been a slave and cruelly treated, but my grandfather loved her and made her his wife. She never forgot her people, the Kai, and she told me of the legend, which was told to her by her mother. The legend is very old. No one knows its age or its beginning."

"Tell us the story Grandmother," Jonti said.

Sayo closed her eyes and looked into her memory, seeking the voice from long ago. "The Kai once walked with The One Spirit who is the maker of all. In those times there was no hunger or pain or war. The Kai were rulers of all, and all was well with their world, but they angered The One Spirit and could walk with him no more. The One Spirit was replaced by many, bringing pain, sorrow, and war. Great darkness surrounded them. Fear and hopelessness walked with them, and then the promise was given." She opened her eyes and looked squarely at Sierra.

Chapter 10

"What promise Grandmother?" Jonti urged her to continue as the four listeners waited raptly.

"A nyonya will come and show the Kai the way to walk again with The One Spirit. The nyonya is called Lady of the Dawn because she will bring light back to the Kai as surely as the dawn brings light to the day."

"Ah, I see why my words helped you remember." Jonti nodded in understanding.

"Yes, Grandson. Your words were no accident." She reached a frail hand to touch Sierra's arm. "You will know my people by their sign, the sun on the horizon."

"I seem to be missing something here, Grandmother of my heart. How are these stories connected to Sierra?" Josh had listened to the legend with growing trepidation, especially when he heard the connection to the Kai. They were cannibals and headhunters. As a child he was repeatedly warned not to venture alone far from the village; many who ignored this warning disappeared, never to be seen again.

Sayo turned her dark gaze from his worried frown to rest on the red hair and bright blue eyes of the foreign woman. "The nyonya is called Lady of the Dawn for another reason. She will have hair like the clouds lit by the rising sun and eyes like the sky that surrounds them."

"Stop looking so stunned," Josh said as Prince and his taxi carried them rapidly back toward the city. "It's just an old native legend, and it can't possibly be referring to you."

"What do you mean?" Sierra said, and started to turn towards him, but the cab swerved around a pedestrian, missing him by inches, gluing her eyes to the road.

He smiled, feeling confident after his reassessment of the situation. "Grandmother Sayo said the lady would be a nyonya, and I'm quite positive you're not."

"But they called me nyonya several times today. Just what exactly does that word mean?"

"In casual reference it means your woman. That's the way my friends were referring to you. I think you gathered that much."

"Yes I did. But I'm not 'your woman'. You should've explained that to them. I would've done so myself, but I didn't want to make an unpleasant scene. They're such nice people. I wonder if they're aware of your lifestyle in the States." She shot him a glance, but he seemed not to be bothered in the least by the comment.

The taxicab careened down the bumpy road, oblivious to the other vehicles. Her grip tightened on the back of the seat. "Prince, could you slow down please?"

The driver caught her gaze in the rearview mirror and smiled. "Of course."

"You're wasting your breath," Josh said in a low voice. "He'll slow down for a few moments, and then he'll be right back up to this speed again. They drive this way all the time. Old habits are hard to break, you know," he said and grinned. "Relax, we'll be at the restaurant shortly."

"Restaurant? Why are we going there?" She frowned at him.

"I need to pick something up from there," he replied, and then quickly redirected the conversation. "You really don't need to worry about that old legend."

"I'm not worried. If anything, I'm intrigued, and I don't understand why you're so certain the lady of the legend is not me. You can't be sure simply by that meaning of the word. It seems too vague to me."

"That's true, if that were the only meaning of the word." White teeth flashed in his tanned face, and he laughed.

The knowledge that his amusement was at her expense made her ire rise. "I want you to know, Mr. McCabe, that you're the most insufferable man I've ever met. And I don't appreciate your playing word games at my expense, and besides, did it ever occur to you that I believe Grandmother Sayo because I know something you don't?"

The taxi came to a skidding halt in front of the restaurant. "This could take a few minutes," Josh said. "Keep the meter running."

While Sierra watched Josh walk toward the restaurant, she remembered the question she wanted to ask Prince about his Arabic prayer. She turned her attention to the driver, hoping he didn't think her horribly rude. "Prince, I heard you praying in Arabic, and I'm weak in that language, but I thought you were praising Jesus."

Prince reached inside his shirt collar and pulled out a cross on a chain. "The greatest symbol of freedom."

Sierra's eyes widened. "Are you—?"

"Yes, Miss Evans. I'm a Christian. My mother was Muslim and my father was Hindu. From them I learned to love God and man. I also learned that in order to be one with God, I must be very, very good. The Apostle Paul and I have a great deal in common in our efforts to be good. I despaired until I met Jesus. Now I love God and man, but best of all, I know how much God loves me." He lifted the cross and looked at it. "This much."

Sierra's curiosity still wasn't satisfied. "But Prince, since you're a Christian, why do you pray like a Muslim?"

He smiled, that serene and welcoming smile that radiated peace. "Isn't it appropriate to bow before God? I also go to the Hindu temple and the Mosque regularly. Again, I follow the example of Paul; many people there love God and want to get closer to Him. I do my best to help them."

Sierra smiled and touched the cabby's shoulder. "God bless you in all your efforts for Him."

A movement by the restaurant door caught Sierra's eye and her smile faded. Josh pulled the restaurant door closed, extracted a key from his pocket and locked it, leaving Sierra wondering why Josh would have a key to Jonti's restaurant. She didn't wonder long.

Josh turned, carrying his suitcase. When he'd stowed it in the trunk and taken his seat again, she raised her eyebrows and stared at him with a calculating look. Bits and pieces of information formed a suspicion in her mind.

"You're the co-owner of the restaurant, right?" she demanded, and her fingernails tapped an erratic tempo on the seat.

"Nosey little thing, aren't you?"

She ignored his evasion of the question and continued putting pieces together. "There's an office with a place to sleep, right?"

"Maybe." Josh leaned with nonchalance against the seat and returned her stare.

"You knew all along that we didn't need two rooms, didn't you?"

"Maybe."

"Answer me! You knew and you were just, just…oh, you creep!" She clenched her fists until the color fled, but it flew to her cheeks making them flame brighter than her hair.

Raphael and Zephon followed this exchange from outside the cab. "Why is God allowing this testing of them, Raphael?"

"You will see." He cast a glance her way, but continued his protective observation.

I don't like what I see so far. Zephon admitted to herself.

Josh lifted an eyebrow. "If you tell me your secret, I'll tell you mine."

Sierra couldn't believe his audacity, and she gave him a vindictive little smile. "I refuse to tell you my secret, Mr. McCabe, and I already know yours, so don't speak to me at all unless it's to apologize."

"What is this Mr. McCabe stuff? At Jonti's house you called me Josh."

Sierra wondered if he was selectively deaf, but she felt compelled to defend herself. "That was a mere slip of the tongue. After all, your friends were calling you by your first name."

"We could be friends." He smiled, but it didn't reach his eyes.

The suggestive tone of his statement made her squirm in her seat. "We haven't known each other long enough to truly be friends. True friendship takes time and trust. It's obvious that we have very little of either."

"What makes you think we have so little time? I know I said this was only a visit to my parents, but I never said how long. I could stay indefinitely. I'm always welcome in my parents' home." He crossed his arms, leaned back and stared at her like a bug under a microscope.

She stiffened her spine, and her teeth clenched. "I'm sure your parents would like it very much if you could lengthen your visit," she replied, forcing herself to answer with a calm voice. She didn't want to dwell on the possibility of Josh extending his stay, so she attempted to change the subject. "You inferred earlier that there's a more formal meaning for the word nyonya. I'd like to know what it is please."

So would I. Zephon's thoughts echoed Sierra's, but they were both forced to wait as the taxi had arrived at the airport.

In the waiting room later, Sierra determined to get a reply, even if it required bribery. She had noticed his taste for strong coffee during their meals together, so the coffee kiosk presented the perfect opportunity. She presented it to him with a charming smile, followed shortly by the question.

Josh recognized her tactic. With great restraint, he held back the urge to chuckle, fearing any levity would set off the temper that definitely went with the hair. He stalled.

"Well?" She allowed him only a sip of his coffee.

Like a schoolboy reciting from his Dani dictionary, he quoted, "Nyonya is a female of childbearing age who belongs to a man."

"Belongs to? You mean, she is owned, like a possession?"

"Not exactly," he hedged.

"What exactly do you mean then?"

"It means she belongs to him physically, as in mated to him."

"Oh." A soft sound escaped her when she absorbed the implications of this.

"And since you are definitely a…uh."

The look of outrage on her face stopped the word before it was formed. To placate her, he tried to explain. "So you see, you can't be the lady of the legend because you've never..."

"Mr. McCabe," she interrupted, "this subject is none of your business." She turned away from him, reached for her carryon and extracted her Bible from its depths. "If you don't mind, I'd like to have some quiet time." She opened her Bible, turned her back to him, and retreated into peace.

He frowned at the Bible in her hands and walked away, sipping his coffee, and mumbling to himself, "What a buffoon you are McCabe. You really bumbled that one. But I know I'm right." Without conscious thought his route took him in a circle back to Sierra. She had adjusted her chair, turning a partial profile to him. The soft light from the window outlined the delicate curve of her jaw and reflected off the shine of her hair like tiny sparks from a well-laid fire. So absorbed was she that she didn't hear his approach and jumped, startled from her concentration.

"I'm sorry. I didn't mean to frighten you," he said.

"Well, it's several weeks late, but I accept your apology," she replied, purposely mistaking his meaning.

His eyes narrowed as he realized what she referred to. "That isn't what I was apologizing for, and you know it."

"That's too bad, Mr. McCabe, because you do still owe me an apology for that."

"I can't apologize for the kiss. But I am sorry *if* you were afraid." He stressed the if as though he doubted its truthfulness.

"I can assure you that it was a very frightening experience for me."

He shook his head. "You didn't feel afraid when you were in my arms. You felt—" He stopped and turned away. "Never mind."

Sierra's emotions seesawed like she had been given a beautifully wrapped box that was empty inside. The intense desire for him to finish what he had begun to say startled her.

"Do you always do that?" he asked, pulling her away from examining her reaction.

She gave him a puzzled look. "Do what?"

"Read your Bible twice a day. You read it twice today and yesterday."

Joy sprang from her heart like bubbles from a child's toy pipe. *This is a good sign, Lord, that he has opened the subject. Please give me wisdom and the right words to say.* "I try to be quotidian about it. It's like food for the soul, so I usually read my Bible at least once a day. Twice a day when I'm in trying circumstances."

"And you find being with me very trying, is that it?" he asked, a thread of pain in the harshness of his statement.

"No, that is, it's the whole experience of going to a foreign country as a missionary. Not just you." Sierra wanted to slap herself the moment the last three words left her mouth. *Oh, darn my wayward tongue. Sorry, Lord, this isn't going well.* "What I mean is," she tried again, "I read my Bible because I want to grow to be more like Jesus, and God's word is food to help me grow."

"You're very naïve, Sierra. You think by being a good little Christian by your example, I'll come back to Him. Well, I won't. I've been down that road, and I don't like where it leads. Besides, don't you know that the more you give, the more He asks of you?"

She blinked away the quick tears that sprang to her eyes. "You may think me naïve, but I'm willing to give whatever He asks and go wherever He asks."

Any reply from Josh was forestalled by the crackle of the loudspeaker, announcing that their flight to Sentani was ready.

CHAPTER 11

The two angels landed at the Sentani air field, folded their wings, and watched the arrival of the plane carrying Josh and Sierra. The immediate area showed no sign of the enemy, but they detected a sulphurous stench, a sure indicator of recent activity.

The plane bounced when the tires touched down on the runway; its speed decreased with a screech and a loud gust of air.

Sierra took a deep breath, stretched and exhaled, endeavoring to encourage her circulation. The five-hour flight to Sentani on the small jet had left her stiff.

"I'd dearly love to go for a walk. My muscles are screaming for motion."

Josh stood and allowed her to proceed him down the isle. "There won't be time for that. Pete and I'll be loading the plane for take off as soon as possible. It's a two-hour flight to the mission station, and we have to arrive before dark. It's too dangerous to land in the jungle at night. If it's exercise you want, you're going to love tomorrow. We have a seven hour hike ahead of us to reach the village." He stepped around her and waved at a smiling, sandy-headed man in a Dodgers cap who approached them.

Raphael and Zephon joined Zuriel, the angel who walked at the man's side. "The enemy's been here. Have you encountered him?" Raphael hurried to ask.

"Yes. A demon of sabotage appeared near our aircraft, but I

dispatched him quickly." The burly, brown-haired, angel replied, but diligently watched his charge's every step as he crossed the tarmac.

"Hello Pete," Josh said, and grabbed the pilot's hand. "It's good to see you. This is Sierra Evans." He nodded towards her. "Sierra, Pete Alexander, the best jungle pilot I've ever met. Pete and his wife, Cheryl, run the mission station at Kokonau."

"Pleased to meet you Miss Evans." The soft southern drawl gave lie to the impression generated by his ball cap.

She shook his work-roughened hand. "Your accent is a surprise. I expected you to be from the Los Angeles area, judging by your hat."

"No ma'am, I'm from San Antoine. But I did a stint in the Navy and was stationed in Southern California. The Dodgers were playing some mighty good ball then. This cap is just a little souvenir. I can tell by that accent, you're from the old Lone Star State too."

"Yes, I am. I spent most of my life on my grandmother's farm outside of Dallas. It's nice to find a fellow Texan way out here."

A hardy chuckle shook his tall thin frame. "Sometimes I have to pinch myself to make sure I'm not imagining this myself. I never figured when I was crop dusting back home in San Antoine, or flying choppers in the Navy, I'd ever be a missionary pilot in the jungle; but I went to a Billy Graham crusade meeting one night, and God got hold of my heart, and here I am. There was nobody more surprised by it than me. But I'll tell you the truth, Miss Evans, there ain't no place on earth I'd rather be right now than right here serving the Lord."

"I know exactly what you mean," Sierra said and nodded. "I feel the same way Mr. Alexander, and please call me Sierra."

"Why thank you ma…Sierra. I will if you'll call me Pete."

"I hate to break up your party here," Josh said gruffly, "but I think I see the boxes of supplies being ferried over to the plane. We better get moving if we're going to get to the station tonight."

"Hey, buddy, you're right about that." Pete's lanky frame covered the distance in long strides as all three of them walked to the other plane. "Whoa, that's a whole heap of stuff you've got there." He pushed back his cap and scratched his head in doubt. "I got a bad feeling about this," he said, staring at the heavily laden trundle.

"Oh dear, is there a problem?" Sierra asked with a gathering brow.

"Could be a little one if my guess is right," he said. "But don't you worry; we'll work it out if there is one. What was the total weight of all this stuff?"

"It came to nine hundred eighty seven pounds," Josh said.

A long whistle followed this announcement. Pete shook his head. "I was afraid of that. It won't all fit in the hold. We'll have to leave some of it here, but it's only for one night. I'll come back tomorrow and get the rest." He and Josh loaded the heavy boxes, and after making the necessary arrangements to store the remainder of the shipment in a safe place until the following day, they took off.

The three angels flew alongside the plane, glad to be in the air, away from the enemy's stench, and in a blue sky that gave no cover to attackers. Against the sky, their wings glowed in rainbow iridescence as they moved with effortless grace.

"Whew!" Pete shoved back his cap and wiped a perspiring forehead. "I sure am glad to be up outta that heat and humidity. I praise the Lord every time I go down to the lowlands that the mission station is located in a highland valley where the weather is more pleasant." As he spoke he banked the small plane, turning gently over the coastline, and brought them around to head towards the interior.

They headed straight for the mountains, and the steamy coastline gave way to gentle hills. Cruising along the coastal mountains that led into a valley with a clear blue ribbon of water winding its way through the lush greenness and glinting like a mirror in the sun, the plane passed through mist that hovered like an ever-present ghost over each emerald green valley as they drew nearer the towering cloud shrouded peaks. With confident skill, Pete banked the small aircraft often, following the landmark waterway's flow from the rain-washed heights.

Sierra's eyes feasted on the panorama below. The blues and greens in every shade, artfully painted by a genius beyond imagination, left her awed and filled her heart and soul with wonder. In her enchantment, she failed to notice the withdrawal of her reluctant escort.

Pete and Sierra continued in conversation, but to Josh, their voices blended into the engine's drone. Depression settled over him, darkening his face like the cloud covered mountain because his thoughts had gone back in time, tearing open a rabid wound. Without success, he tried to push the image from his mind. He barely heard most of their conversation during the flight, but their comments about the beauty of Irian Jaya broke through his reverie, and he couldn't help but agree—Irian is wild and beautiful—but it will steal your heart and repay your love with treachery and pain.

"There she is." Pete whooped. "Home, sweet home. Welcome to Black Hills Mission Station, Sierra." He circled the plane lower over a high plateau, and the buildings of the station came into view as they approached a landing strip.

Mountains hedged the wide green expanse of the plateau on three sides, and provided ample foliage where native huts nestled in the trees as though floating on the treetops, daring gravity to destroy their birdlike perches. When the noise of the plane engine signaled its approach, the natives seemed to swarm out of the jungle, running with smiling brown faces to line the landing strip. A cheer of welcome muted the sound of the plane's engine.

"Do they always welcome you home so exuberantly?" A smile lit Sierra's face in response to the unrestrained joy of the natives.

"No. This welcome is not for me; it's for you and especially for Josh. He's a real favorite around here. That's all they've been talking about for days now. Tuan Josh is coming and bringing his nyonya."

"But I'm not…"

"Yeh, I know." Pete grinned sheepishly. "But once they heard Josh was bringing a young woman, they put their own definition on it. There's the rest of our welcoming party now, my wife Cheryl." He nodded towards a smiling fair-haired lady who waved a greeting and ran to meet them. He taxied the plane to a stop and cut the engine before jumping out to embrace his wife.

Before Sierra could react, Josh exited the plane, opened her door, and reached his hands toward her waist as though to lift her down from the plane. He stopped, dropped one hand and offered the other. But Sierra appeared not to notice. Her eyes and ears remained fixed on the sea of dark smiling faces that surrounded the plane and them, and a chorus of voices that chattered excitedly. She climbed down from the plane without assistance and the natives closed around her. An occasional word of English jumped out at her from the smiling faces.

But not all the faces smiled. Raphael drew his sword in a flash of light when he detected a native surging through the crowd with a group of demons attached to his back. Zephon spotted the intruder at almost the same instant, and her blade sang with power at its release from her scabbard. The demons screeched in defiance. Zuriel and Cheryl's guardian, Rainiel, along with the guardians of many of the natives, rushed to their aid with swords ready. Seeing their target so well protected, the demons flung curses at their opponents, but spun their captive around and sent him running toward the jungle.

Feeling overwhelmed by the strangeness of her new surroundings, and a sudden tide of heaviness that pressed on her spirit, Sierra heaved a sigh of relief when the crowd parted to allow Pete and his wife to join them.

"Sierra, this is Cheryl." The pilot smiled and squeezed his wife to his side.

"It's wonderful to meet you," Cheryl said, and took Sierra's hand. "I'm so looking forward to your visit. Come on up to the house." She stopped speaking to return a quick hug from Josh.

Cheryl's warm brown eyes, honey blond hair, and smile that flashed dimples in both cheeks reminded Sierra of an adult version of Shirley Temple, and a clear musical voice completed the illusion.

Zephon and Rainiel followed the two women, keeping a sharp eye out for any more enemies. Zephon's hand still rested on her sword hilt as she addressed Cheryl's guardian. "Do you experience that type of attack often?"

"No." Rainiel replied with a reassuring smile. "The majority of our natives walk with the Lord now. That's the first in a long time. The enemy senses the movement of God's hand I believe." She looked toward the two women who had just reached the house and nodded at Sierra.

It was a long walk, and Sierra enjoyed the opportunity to get her circulation moving. Set on a small hill above the airfield, the house was constructed of prefabricated aluminum and appeared larger than she had expected.

Cheryl proudly showed her the great-room with adjoining kitchen and five bedrooms, all decorated in tropical colors, complete with wallpaper and borders. "The station was designed as a stopover for missionaries in route to and from their assigned areas," she explained, "so we have extra bedrooms. A team came from my church and did all the painting and decorating. Oh my, here I am jabbering away and running you around when you'd probably like nothing more than to sit down with a cold drink and rest."

"No really," Sierra reassured her. "I've been sitting for so long, it feels good to walk around. But I would like a cold drink."

"Come on in the kitchen and I'll get us tall glasses of tea and some sandwiches." She led the way back through the station. "Those men should be coming in any time now. I'll bet they'd like some too." She motioned for Sierra to sit. "Is that a Texas accent I heard? I can't believe the Lord would really bless me with a visit from someone from home."

Sierra grinned. "Yes, I'm from the Dallas area. Pete said you grew up there."

Cheryl chuckled. "I love it. Not only from Texas but from Dallas too. I thought I recognized that accent, but I wondered if my imagination was playing tricks on me cause I've been out here so long." She filled a tray with four frosty mugs of tea, sandwiches, and cookies and brought it to the table.

"How long have you been here?" Sierra lifted her glass and sipped the cold, refreshing liquid.

"Almost four years this time. We're due for a home assignment in three months. I can't wait. I guess you can tell, huh?"

"Don't you like it here?"

She smiled wistfully. "I love it, actually. I love the island, and the people have captured my heart. Pete and I have both fallen in love with them. It gives me a feeling that's hard to describe when we have Sunday services, and I see the people praising and worshiping God. They are so unreserved in their joy of the Lord. God has done a miracle here. Only a few years ago these people lived in fear of evil spirits. I consider myself very blessed to be able to help bring salvation to the many other tribes. But sometimes I get so homesick I could cry." Tears brightened her eyes when she said this last. "But don't tell Pete."

Sierra's hand reached out to clasp Cheryl's. "Don't worry, I won't tell."

"Hey, won't tell what?" Pete echoed as he and Josh strode through the door. "You ladies sharing secrets already?"

"Of course." Cheryl stood and handed the men each a cold mug and sandwich laden plate.

"Hey, thanks." Pete took a long drink before continuing. "Boy, is this welcome. Lifting all those heavy boxes works up a powerful thirst. If you ladies don't mind, me and Josh are fixing to go back down to the hanger. We've got some work to do on the plane to get it ready for the return trip to fetch the rest of your supplies tomorrow. We're just gonna eat and get right back to it. I'm sure you have lots of woman stuff to talk about anyway."

"That's fine, hon. You guys go on. If we've already turned in for the night when you get back, I've put Josh in the blue room and Sierra in the green, so you'll know who goes where."

"Okay, we'll see you all later." Pete headed out the door with Josh close behind. "Whoa," Pete yelled as the door was closing. "Cheryl, honey," the pilot said as he stuck his head back in the door. "You otta bring Sierra out here on the porch. There's gonna be a beautiful sunset. She's getting a fine welcome to Irian."

"Thanks sweetheart. We'll be there in a minute."

Coral flames arched across the sky when the two ladies emerged onto the wide covered porch. A warm glow bathed the green plateau as the clouds transformed against the sapphire sky. A gentle breeze blew strands of Sierra's hair softly against her cheeks. Only an occasional birdcall interrupted the peaceful setting. The beauty and serenity of the moment transported Sierra. It took her a moment to come back from the little bit of heaven. "Are the sunsets always this beautiful?" she asked quietly.

"No. Pete's right. God's giving you a special welcome. I'm glad the men will be gone for a while tomorrow. That will give us time for a nice long talk. I have something important I want to tell you."

Chapter 12

"Look out pancakes. Here we come." Pete's and Cheryl's voices heralded their arrival to the kitchen the next morning.

"Oh my, Sierra," Cheryl adjusted the collar of her yellow housedress. "This looks wonderful. You should have let me help you. I feel like such a lazy bones, lying in bed till this hour." She took the seat Pete pulled out for her.

"Let's pray quick," Pete said, hitching his chair up to the table. "My mouth is watering so hard, it's about to wash my teeth right outta my mouth. Lord, we sure do thank you for this beautiful day and this good food. Please keep Josh and I safe as we go fetch the rest of those supplies, and keep the ladies safe while we're gone. Thank you Jesus, amen." Rubbing his hands together in anticipation, he reached for the pancakes.

"You'd think I never feed him, the way he carries on." Cheryl scolded good-naturedly.

"She feeds me plenty. I was just born with a hollow leg, my momma used to say. Always had a hearty appetite, especially in the mornings." Pete heaped several pancakes in a pile on his plate and handed the platter to Josh before reaching for the syrup.

Sierra ate quietly, observing how her new friends exchanged playful gibes. Their love for each other radiated warmth like the sun streaming in the windows. *Please Lord. That's the kind of marriage I want. Give me someone special who will be my best friend as well as my husband.* Resolutely, she refused to look at Josh, sure that he was not the one God had planned for her.

Wiping the moisture from the last dish, Sierra placed it in the cabinet and folded the towel over the bar to dry, then she pulled on the bow at the back of her waist and removed the patchwork apron, returning it to its place in the cupboard. The mission kitchen was quiet except for the sound of life—the song of birds and the voices of playing native children—that drifted in the open windows. The men had left promptly after breakfast, and Sierra had chased Cheryl from the kitchen, proclaiming a morning of rest for her. A gentle melody of praise floated in on the breeze and announced her location. Cheryl sat on her front porch, a basket of mending beside her.

"You're supposed to be having a little vacation from work." Sierra scolded as she stepped through the screen door and spotted her friend.

Zephon followed Sierra and went to stand by Rainiel on the porch.

"I am." Cheryl said and laughed. "But I have to keep my hands busy. Come and sit down here." She indicated a chair next to her. "Isn't this a beautiful morning?"

"It is." Sierra made herself comfortable, smoothing the long skirt of her blue dress. Only a few puffy clouds dotted the sky so bright sunlight bathed the plateau where native children played while their parents worked at various tasks.

Cheryl looked up from her mending to meet Sierra's eyes in a searching look. "Have you known Josh long?"

Sierra leaned away from Cheryl, momentarily speechless.

"I'm sorry" Cheryl said, "I sound terribly nosy, but I'm concerned. You see, we've known him a long time, and he's been through a lot. I've noticed how he looks at you. I think he likes you a lot, and I'm wondering how you feel about him."

Zephon didn't relax in her watchfulness, but her ears perked up at their topic.

Catching her breath, Sierra was not sure how to respond; she looked up at the deep green mountains, unable to meet Cheryl's probing gaze. "I'm sure you've misread things. Mr. McCabe and I have only known each other a short time."

"No, I don't think so. I know Josh pretty well I think. The question is—how do you feel about him?"

With a sigh, Sierra admitted, "I honestly don't know. There's something wrong between Josh and God. I can't let myself care about him until that conflict's resolved. Since I was eight years old I've been determined to be a missionary. I can't let anything interfere with that, not even Josh. It's too important. You can understand that, can't you?" She leaned toward her hostess.

A slow smile turned up the corners of Cheryl's mouth. "Yes, but you already do care about him. Maybe I can help you to understand him better. He and his older brother and little sister grew up here in Irian Jaya. Their parents were Bible translators to the Dani for almost twenty years."

"Yes. I knew that. I met Jonti and Kimi and Grandmother Sayo in Jakarta."

"Oh, did you? Aren't they wonderful? How is the orphanage doing?"

"Orphanage?"

"Oh, you didn't hear about that. Jonti and Josh support a Christian orphanage in Jakarta with the income from their restaurant. You did visit the restaurant?"

"Yes, it was very beautiful. Josh did mention an orphanage, but only in passing, and not in connection with himself." She paused, digesting this new evidence about Josh.

Cheryl looked up from the button she was sewing on a shirt. "Okay, so you know Josh had a brother and sister."

"Had? Oh no. Something happened to them?"

"Yes. Five years ago Josh's older brother went into the mountains of Irian as a language surveyor. Only a native guide accompanied him and another missionary. The two missionaries were slaughtered by an extremely primitive tribe. Only the guide escaped."

Sierra gasped and covered her mouth with her hand. She closed her eyes, but tears seeped through her lashes and stopped her voice.

"It was very hard for all of them," Cheryl whispered, "but especially for Josh. He idolized his older brother."

"And yet his parents continue to work here?" Sierra looked up, wiping at the moisture on her cheeks.

Cheryl nodded. "Jim and Elizabeth McCabe have a deep and abiding faith in God and a solid conviction that this is were God wants them to serve Him."

Sierra remembered her mother and father before the accident. The old pain tore at her heart.

"I don't think Josh ever got over the loss of his brother, though; and less than two years later, his little sister died also."

"Not the natives again?" Sierra asked, and her stomach somersaulted.

"No. Thank goodness. She died from a ruptured appendix. She'd been in pain for several days without telling anyone, and when she finally did, it was too late to get her off the mountain. The only way in and out is on foot, and it's much too slow in an emergency. I'm afraid it was all too much for Josh. He's been angry at God ever since. He adored his little sister."

Tears coursed down Sierra's cheeks. "Excuse me." She wiped them away again and blinked back more.

"It's all right. I've cried rivers for all of them myself. Now can you understand Josh a little better?"

"Yes. Thank you for telling me. What amazing people his parents must be."

"They're very special. You're going to love them. Would you like to go for a walk now and limber up your legs before the long hike tomorrow?"

"I'd love to." Sierra stood and stretched her lethargic muscles. As they left the shady porch and stepped into the sunshine, she pondered all that Cheryl had told her. *Father in heaven, please help Josh to heal from the loss of his brother and sister. Please make his pain go away. Help him to trust you once again.*

Tears sparkled in Zephon's eyes, and a great wave of remorse washed over her. *Forgive me, Lord, for my bad attitude toward*

Joshua McCabe. He's your child, and you sit as a refiner and purifier with your eye on him in the flames, in order to make him an image of yourself. Your will be done, even if it involves Sierra.

"Have you ever hiked for seven hours before?" Josh demanded in frustration at her stubbornness.

"Don't take that tone with me, Mr. McCabe. The answer to your question is no, but I'm very strong and perfectly capable of carrying a backpack. I'd appreciate it if you'd let me help. Especially since one of the porters is sick, and we're short a man. If I help, than it'll be easier to divide the remaining weight among the others without overloading anyone." Sierra's attitude toward Josh had softened since her conversation with Cheryl, but his dictator ways raised her ire.

"What she says makes a lot of sense buddy," Pete said. "Besides, you can keep an eye on her to make sure she's not wearing down too fast."

"All right." Josh threw his hands up. "But she'll be sorry."

"Don't worry, Mr. McCabe. You won't hear a word of complaint from me." She hefted the half-full backpack onto her khaki clad shoulders and fastened the buckles as she had seen the native porters do. "There, that isn't too heavy for me."

"We'll see," Josh replied, tucking his white camp shirt into gray shorts before hefting his own pack.

Cheryl blinked back tears and hugged Sierra. "You take care now. I hope I'll see you again sometime. We'll be gone on home assignment before you come down the mountain again. God bless you and guide you always."

"Thank you. We'll call you on the radio to let you know we've arrived safely. Good-by." Sierra returned her hug with real affection and a sense of loss that they wouldn't see each other again for a long time. She turned away and followed the convoy of natives who headed toward the towering mountains.

"Good-by ole buddy." Pete clasped his friend's hand and gave him a one armed hug. "We'll be seeing you in a few weeks when your visit's over. You just let me know when to expect you."

"I'll do that. Thanks for everything. You guys are the best." Josh waved a last farewell before he set off in long strides to catch the line of hikers who moved at a steady pace toward the first mountain pass.

Raphael took wing. Flying in slow circles over the hikers, he nodded to Zephon and several other guardians, taking note of the size of their force.

The jungle thickened rapidly when they left the plateau behind, and the day that had dawned bright and clear unraveled into gloom, made oppressive by gray clouds that gathered on the mountain peaks, making the air sticky, and the shadows forbidding. The trail narrowed; in places it became almost impassable because of the encroaching greenery, winding slowly up, and then down, and then up again. The forest was alive with the sound of birds. Bright darts of color signaled the location of a flock of lorries; their fifing call filled the air when they rose in alarm at the unexpected intruders. The path wound higher. The heat increased while the morning wore on, and the number and variety of insects seemed to increase in direct proportion to the heat.

Sierra found herself waving her hands repeatedly to chase the pests from swarming in front of her face, and she thanked God for insect repellent that kept them from biting. When the backpack became heavier with each step, she began to see the folly in her stubbornness. With only an occasional stop for a sip of water, they had been hiking for a little over three hours when she felt she could go no farther without a rest.

"Are you tired?" Josh echoed her thoughts as though he had read her mind.

"A little. Are we going to stop soon for lunch?" She looked back over her shoulder to where Josh walked behind her. A rock in the path caught her toe, causing her to stumble and fall backwards from the weight of the pack.

Strong arms closed around her, and he stepped back to absorb the momentum of her fall. "You *are* tired," he said in a gentle voice and felt her tremble.

She straightened away from him. "Thank you. You saved me from a nasty fall. I'll have to watch my step more carefully." She refused to look at him, aware that her pulse raced from more than her stumble.

"You'll be able to rest soon. We should hear the waterfall anytime now."

No sooner had he spoken than they rounded a turn in the path, and a low rumble could be heard, its volume increasing with every few steps.

Sierra listened in awe. The sound became louder until she not only heard it, but she felt it; the very ground vibrated with the waterfall's pounding, and the air was filled with a cool mist, diminishing the heat and even the bugs. Then she saw it. A break in the foliage at the side of the trail framed a postcard perfect scene where the giant waterfall cascaded and crashed onto huge rocks, and lush ferns hugged the shore, their feathery leaves shining with moisture in the sunshine that had conquered the clouds.

On a signal from their leader, the meandering line of porters stopped, and everyone removed their heavy backpacks, quickly shedding their weight. Lunches were brought out, and they all sank to the ground.

Sierra ate hurriedly, an idea forming in her mind. She stood up and stared at the view, her eyes scanning the surrounding jungle, then turned to face Josh. "It's bigger than it looks, isn't it? I want to go closer and see the true size. Is there a trail?"

He nodded. "There's a trail, but it's dangerous. You can't go over there by yourself. Forget it." As if that was the end of the subject, he went back to his lunch.

"Then I'll find someone to go with me." She moved to carry out her plan.

"Wait!" Josh stood up, brushing the crumbs from his shorts, a look of annoyance on his face. "I'll show you how big it is." Pointing to a spot directly in front of the view, he commanded, "Stay here and watch the waterfall."

"But what…?"

"Just watch, you'll see." He insisted, and then he disappeared through a wall of plants with Raphael at his side.

Sierra caught glimpses of Josh through the trees, and she realized he was making his way closer to the water, then she lost sight of him in the jungle. Her heart began to pound. She wondered if it was truly dangerous, and her frightened eyes fastened on the thundering water, concerned that he was in trouble when he didn't reappear. Then a tiny figure stepped onto a large flat boulder that rose above the foaming pool of water at the base of the waterfall and waved its arms. With arms upraised, she signaled in return. Her eyes looked slowly from him to the top of the waterfall and back again, and an "Oh" of astonishment escaped her when she realized the immensity of the cascading water. The man gave perspective to the true size, which she had only guessed at before. She stared, hardly blinking, her heart lifted up to God for creating such a magnificently beautiful sight. Just a few minutes later, he melted into the trees again, taking what seemed an inordinate amount of time to reappear by her side.

She turned pleading eyes on him. "I want to get closer, please?"

He gave her a crooked little smile and said, "Be careful what you ask for."

She stamped her foot when she realized his intentional misinterpretation of her request. "I meant to the waterfall, and you know it."

Against his better judgement, he yielded to her request and led her through the dense plants to a narrow trail. The sound grew louder until it was deafening when they reached the edge of the foaming pool where he stopped. "You can't go any further. The rocks are slippery."

"But you did. If you can do it, so can I." She started past him.

"You stubborn woman. Alright," he said, and grabbed her hand. "Hold on now and watch your step." Josh warned, his mouth close to her ear, and his grip on her hand tightened. He led her carefully from rock to rock, and stopped on the one from which he had signaled to Sierra, then he assisted her to join him, making sure her feet where stable on the mist and moss slick rock. She lifted her eyes, and his followed hers to the top.

Raphael and Zephon spread their wings in the mist and fluttered them gently, like birds at their bath. Zephon allowed a trill to escape her; like wind chimes in a gentle breeze, it charmed the ears of the humans and then blended into the roar of the water.

The sun shone through the mist making a rainbow that seemed to arch toward Josh and Sierra. Tiny drops of moisture glistened on their hair and skin. The power and beauty of the water surrounded them, and the rest of the world receded.

Sierra's head turned towards Josh, and her heart did a little tap-dance in her chest as she stared into his handsome face, but she reminded herself of his attitude toward God, and with all the resolve she had, she pulled herself back to reality.

"Thank you for sharing this with me. I knew it would be even more beautiful up close," she said, forced to put her lips near his ear so she could be heard over the thunderous crash of the falls.

"Don't fall in love with Irian Jaya, Sierra. It's a twisted lover who'll lead you on, then stab you in the back."

His breath was warm on her skin, but cold shivers ran down her spine. Almost robbed of her joy in the beautiful spot, she turned toward the waterfall once more, shook her head, and then looked back at him. "It's too late. I love it, already. Shouldn't we go back? They're probably ready to get started again."

Josh didn't reply immediately, just continued looking down at her standing so close to him. The moisture on her hair and skin glistened in the sunlight, and in spite of her words, it drew him like an oasis in the desert.

Chapter 13

In the village where James and Elizabeth McCabe worked, Raphael and Zephon quickly made the acquaintance of the guardians, Arioch and Briel, who watched over the missionaries. The four angels stood outside the mission house under a canopy of stars that blazed in unrestrained brilliance in the storm washed sky.

Arioch, a lion-like angel of immense proportions, nodded his head as Raphael related the details of the attempted attack at Black Hills Mission Station. "Yes. I've sensed a stirring in the enemy's camp for many days now. They're up to something."

"We must be ever more vigilant to protect them." Raphael lifted his hand toward the house and its occupants.

Unaware of the plans for her safety, Sierra reclined in a tub full of water. She relaxed in the warm bath and let the stiffness flow out of her sore muscles while her mind wondered, drifting on a haze of total exhaustion, thinking of the McCabe family.

Josh's mother had known immediately that her new assistant was worn out and chilled to the bone from the soaking rain. Without allowing an argument, she ushered her into a hot bath. Elizabeth McCabe had a smile that could melt an iceberg but a will as strong as Sierra herself. James McCabe was a surprise. Meeting him was like looking into the future and seeing Josh as he would appear in thirty years or so. The raven's wing black of Josh's hair was almost white on his father, and the green of James McCabe's eyes presented a striking contrast. A strong jaw and chiseled profile were softened by his boyishly charming smile. The marked difference was their attitude, not appearance; James McCabe had serenity that Sierra knew came from being at one with the will of God. *If only Josh was like his father in that way also, I would...* Her eyes flew open when she realized where her thoughts were leading. She grabbed the soap and began scrubbing.

A knock on the door preceded the voice of her hostess. "Dear, when you're finished, I have some warm soup for your supper. But there's no hurry, unless you're starving."

Sierra's stomach growled at the thought of food. "I'll be right out," she called and finished her bath in a hurry. Donning a robe, she opened the bathroom door to find Elizabeth waiting with a tray from which arose a mouth-watering aroma.

"I thought you might like to eat in your room where you can relax and go right to sleep if you want. That's an extremely exhausting hike up the mountain. I know you must be dead on your feet."

"Thank you. I'm very tired, food and sleep sound like a bit of heaven right now. Is that chicken soup I smell?"

A lighthearted laugh greeted her question. "Not exactly, but it's the Irian Jaya mountain version of chicken soup and very good for just about anything that ails you. I'll let you take this to your room and we'll see you in the morning."

"Thank you. Good night." Sierra took the tray, and held the steaming bowl under her nose, inhaling with relish.

"It's my pleasure, dear. Sleep well."

The sun was shining brightly when Sierra awakened. With a yawn, she looked at her watch, and her eyes widened. "Oh my, I can't believe I slept for fourteen hours straight." She jumped up, and grimaced when her muscles protested. "That's what you get for being such a strong willed female, you dummy. Now you'll probably be sore for days." She mumbled to herself and dressed with as much haste as her muscles would allow, eager to join her host and hostess and began unpacking all the materials she had brought to help them.

Elizabeth McCabe stood at her kitchen sink in front of a window framed by blue gingham curtains. The sun streamed through the window and gilded the dark auburn waves of her hair. Sierra thought it amazing that a woman her age would have so little gray as she noticed a sprinkling only at the temples of Elizabeth's hair when her hostess turned.

"Good morning," Elizabeth said with a smile. "Oh! You look so much better this morning. You were worn out last night. Did you sleep well?"

"Yes." Sierra laughed. "Too well in fact. I don't remember ever sleeping for fourteen hours before." She winced while sitting down at the table where Elizabeth had placed a plate of steaming hot pancakes.

"Are you very stiff and sore today dear?"

"I'm afraid so. That's what I get for being so hardheaded, but I'm sure it'll work out as I move around," she said a quick prayer and attacked the pancakes with a voracious appetite from all the exercise.

"Try rubbing this in where it hurts. I find it works wonders for my sore muscles." Mrs. McCabe placed a jar of salve on the table and, after pouring herself a mug of coffee, took a seat on the other side.

Swallowing the bite she had been chewing, Sierra replied, "Thank you. These pancakes are wonderful. How did you know I like them?"

A twinkle sparkled in Elizabeth's eyes. "Josh told me before he and his father went to work on the landing strip. He said you're an excellent cook."

Sierra blushed and looked down at her plate.

Elizabeth McCabe saw warm color flood her young co-worker's face, and she hid a smile behind her coffee mug. A prayer of praise and thanksgiving and entreaty went up to her Lord that this young lady might be the miracle she and her husband had been praying for. "Have you known Josh very long?" She sat her cup on the table and wrapped both hands around it.

"No. Not long at all."

"Oh? Did Dr. Cook introduce you just before the trip?"

"No. Actually, we met at a party at my cousin's apartment, sort of. He was…" Sierra realized that she couldn't continue without hurting Elizabeth.

"Oh," Elizabeth responded and sighed. "It was not a pleasant encounter. Was it? That's all right. Don't answer. I can see it in your face. I can only apologize for my son. He's had a very difficult time the past few years. He's still struggling. Please forgive him." Tears drowned her warm brown eyes.

Sierra's heart melted at the love and kindness she saw there, and she reached a hand to clasp Elizabeth's. "It's all right. It's forgiven and forgotten. I admire you so much for persevering in this work. This has been a very difficult few years for you also."

"You know the whole story, don't you?" Elizabeth wiped her eyes and gave Sierra a weak smile.

"I think so. Cheryl told me. She wanted me to understand Josh's attitude."

"Pete and Cheryl are wonderful friends. They've been a source of tremendous encouragement to us."

"Don't you sometimes just want to give up and go home to the states?" The young woman asked in wonder.

"No dear. You see Irian *is* our home, and we know that this is where God wants us. We'll remain here as long as the door is open for us to do so."

"That's the way I feel also. Something has been drawing me to this island." Sierra's face brightened with understanding.

Elizabeth squeezed her hand in agreement and smiled. "Then we're in one accord. Now if you're finished with your breakfast, you rub that cream into your sore muscles, and let's unpack those boxes."

Sierra checked the final item off the list as she and her co-translator emptied the last box. "That's everything on your list, Elizabeth."

"I know. It's wonderful. It's a minor miracle in itself to receive everything we asked for with nothing on backorder."

Closing her eyes, the young woman rubbed the small of her back.

"Oh dear," Elizabeth said. "How thoughtless of me. Making you work for hours when you've only just arrived."

"No really," Sierra protested, "it isn't your fault. The soreness is from yesterday, and it's my own stubbornness coming back to haunt me."

"You know, a good long walk usually helps ease my sore muscles. Why don't we walk through the village and I'll introduce you to the natives."

"That sounds wonderful," Sierra replied, and twisted gently from side to side to stretch her back muscles, than followed Elizabeth out the door into the afternoon sunshine. "Oh my goodness, there's a river." Her first view of the area by daylight surprised her not only for the river, which meandered past the village to disappear into the jungle, but also for the size of the open area.

The village lay down the hill from the mission house and, as they strolled towards it, Elizabeth explained that each cluster of huts represented an extended family group comprising not only parents and grandparents, but aunts and uncles also. The round huts of palm thatched bamboo made an irregular circle with a common ground in the center.

On the far side of the village, looking small in the distance, Sierra spied Josh and his father and several natives working vigorously to clear the jungle growth and level the ground. "Oh, is that the landing strip?"

"Yes." Elizabeth nodded, and lifted a hand to acknowledge her husband's wave. She stared at the cleared land, her smile dimmed, and she seemed far away for a moment, but with a shake of her head, she turned back to Sierra. "Come, I'll introduce you to our Indonesian friends."

Most of the men, who were not helping Josh and his father, were on a hunting expedition, which Elizabeth explained could keep them away for days. But Sierra met the village chief and many of the women, who all stared at her hair and eyes, so many that names and faces blended forcing her to try word association to remember even a few. She put a hand to her forehead and closed her eyes when they left the fourth cluster of huts.

The movement caught Elizabeth's eye. "Oh dear. Forgive me, Sierra. That's enough for one day. Now I've not only overworked you, I've given you information overload. Let's head back to the mission house. You can rest, and I can start dinner." She gave Sierra a shoulder hug, and they turned to head back.

But Sierra stopped. "Elizabeth, would it be okay if I just walk around by myself? The exercise is helping my sore muscles."

"Of course, dear. That's fine. Just come on up to the house when you're ready."

Sierra watched her go, then continued her stroll, enjoying the breeze that made the palms sway and small waves on the river ripple toward shore. From pebble size to boulders, rocks lined the shore, providing a playground for the village children, who were busy climbing, throwing, stacking, or diving from them when Sierra approached. One after another the children stopped their activities and stared at her, then some of the youngest begin to cry or run toward the huts. Realizing they were afraid of her, Sierra cried out in their language, "No, please, I won't hurt you." She lifted her hands palms out, but it did no good, once started, the stampede of children rushed by, leaving the area deserted, but for a few older boys.

Dejected for ruining their playtime, she turned and headed away from river, surveying the jungle and the surrounding mountains. In the jungle, not far from the village, two palm trees captured her gaze because they leaned toward each other and intersected, intrigued, she walked toward the almost perfect x, following a barely discernible trail and leaving the village behind.

"Are you crazy?" A male voice demanded.

Sierra jumped, and her hand flew to her heart.

Chapter 14

"Where do you think you're going?" Josh demanded. Grabbing her arm, he spun her to face him.

Sierra pushed his hand away and flung her head up to rebuke him, but the words took wing like frightened birds when she saw his pale face and rigid stance.

Zephon sighed in relief, not even objecting to the rough treatment of her charge, and nodded her head in agreement. "I'd like to know that also."

Sierra stepped back from him and crossed her arms, her sneaker-clad foot begin tapping the ground. "I'm going for a walk. Isn't that obvious, Mr. McCabe?"

"You're going to get yourself killed. Weren't you warned not to go off into the jungle by yourself?"

"Yes," Sierra retorted, pushing the hair away from her reddening cheeks, "but I'm only going there." She pointed to her landmark. "You know, x marks the spot and all that. I've always loved treasure hunt stories." She shrugged her shoulders.

"You're following the wrong trail." Josh shook his head. "You'd have been lost in a matter of minutes." His body had relaxed, but his voice carried a brittle edge.

Her eyes lit up. "You've been there, haven't you? It's something special, like the waterfall, isn't it? I'll bet the path is close by." She stood on her toes, peering into the trees all around them.

Josh grimaced and shook his head. "I suppose it's a waste of time to say forget it?"

She restrained a victorious little smile and nodded.

"Come on and stay close." He led her back toward the village and alongside the jungle for several yards, then turned onto a clearly discernible trail, which marked it well used in a forest that grew rapidly. He stopped on the path and looked around him, his brow furrowed. "Ah, there it is." He pointed.

Following the line he indicated, she saw the two trees leaning toward each other. It was difficult to spot, camouflaged by the multi-shaded green background, unless one knew where to look.

"The path should be right about here." He stepped off the well-worn trail onto a narrow, barely visible, path. An endless variety of jungle vines pushed their way across the thin strip of worn soil. Josh held the branches back when necessary for her to pass by. The trail snaked through the foliage, but always wound back towards the crossing trees.

Sierra looked up and saw the two trees towering against the foliage directly in front of them and ducked her head to avoid a giant tree fern branch that Josh held clear of the path. They entered a small clearing.

She stopped abruptly with a soft, "Oh." Feathery, lace-like, ferns embraced a tranquil forest pool; their branches seemed to caress the small boulders that they grew among. The pool reflected the blue of the sky and the vivid montage of colorful orchids that grew in profusion on the trees, draping to the ground to blend with a carpet of purple orchids that covered the decaying trunks of fallen trees and trailed their brilliant foliage over the ground to the edge of the rocks. Fragrance filled the air. Sierra closed her eyes and breathed deeply, never having experienced anything like it before—vanilla, but with fresh fruit and subtle spices mixed in.

"Are you happy now?" Josh asked.

She tore her eyes away from the visual feast. "It's incredibly beautiful. How did you find this?"

"I saw the crossed trees." He admitted, staring into her eyes for long moments. "They intrigued me too."

She blushed and forced her gaze back to the orchid pool.

"We should go back," he said, but his body moved closer to the pool, advancing carefully through the bed of orchids.

Sierra glanced back the way they had come, thinking his suggestion had merit, then placed her feet in his footprints, taking great care not to crush any of the flowers.

Zephon looked at the isolated spot and listened. Not a sound could be heard from the village. She turned to Raphael, who had watched the unfolding events in silence, and said, "I have a bad feeling about this."

"Yes," Raphael said. "I do also. I'll watch from above. You stay by them." He nodded at the couple who had stopped by a rock formation.

Josh motioned for her to take a seat. "Here, see, the rocks make a natural bench."

"How perfect." Sierra made herself comfortable on the boulder and used another stone as a footrest. "It's just like God arranged a comfortable place for humans to sit and enjoy this beautiful spot. Have you been here often?"

"No." He didn't speak for long moments after the clipped reply. "This place reminds me of a swimming hole I used to visit as a boy. Although my old childhood haunt didn't have all these flowers. We had a lot of fun there."

Sierra had wondered what he was thinking and by his melancholy tone, she knew he must have been remembering his brother and sister.

"You miss them very much. Don't you?" Sierra whispered. He turned slowly to face her. The pain in his eyes echoed in her heart.

"You know about my brother and sister?"

She nodded her head. "Yes, Cheryl told me. She wanted to help me understand your anger."

"And do you?"

"Better than I did before, but not totally I think." She answered honestly. "Do you want to talk about it?"

"What's to talk about? My brother was my hero. He could do

everything better than anyone. He could have been anything he wanted to be. But he loved God and committed himself to serve him. And how does God repay him? By letting him be murdered by the natives he wanted to help. And as if that wasn't enough heartbreak for my family, God struck my sister down too. She was the kindest, most loving person you'd ever want to meet. She died in horrible pain from a ruptured appendix. What kind of God would let that happen to people who love him, Sierra? Explain that to me."

The agony in his plea brought tears to her eyes. "I don't know how to explain it. But God has a plan. I know he does. You have to trust him."

"I don't trust him. I think he sacrifices people for his own purposes without caring about the pain he causes. My brother and sister died for nothing."

"No Josh, you're wrong. They died for the creator of the universe, for the one who is 'from everlasting to everlasting.' If you could ask them, they would tell you there's no greater cause to die for. Please Josh, you've got to let go of the pain. They wouldn't want you to feel this way."

Josh went still. A small gentle voice repeated Sierra's words in his mind and he bowed his head, knowing that she was right.

"Be happy for them Josh, they're with the one they love." Sierra placed her hand on his.

Silence greeted her words. Only the sound of bird song, and a gentle breeze in the treetops could be heard. Josh shook his head, then slowly turned to face her. "Are you with the one you love Sierra? You just spoke my name three times." He took her shoulders in an impassioned grip. "You love me, don't you?"

She had no time to reply as he bent his head to hers. His mouth took possession of hers. His hands moved to bury themselves in the silk of her hair. A feeling of wildfire ran through her body, and her mind spun. She responded to his kiss with urgency.

Zephon drew her blade, sure the enemy must be near. She sensed their presence before she saw them.

Josh released Sierra's lips and trailed kisses across her cheek. "I know you love me. Come away with me. Don't sacrifice yourself here in this jungle because you feel guilty about something that was beyond your control."

His passionate whisper penetrated her mind, bringing her sharply back to reality. "No! You don't know what you're talking about." She pushed away from his arms and stood, backing up against the rocks.

"You love me. I know you do. You melted in my arms just now. Come back to me."

She held up a her hand to ward him off when he made a move toward her. "Stay away from me or I'll scream. I'll not love someone who's angry with God. I'm not here in Irian because of guilt."

Aren't you? A small voice hissed.

Am I? I don't know. She shut her eyes. *God, help me.*

The snake slithered over the rock behind Sierra. The demon under the snake's skin thought himself well camouflaged by the rock's dark color. Like the wind, Zephon swept forward, driving the demon from the serpent's body, her sword a flame of fire, but the demon's influence continued.

The snake raised its venomous head and drew back to strike. The instant Josh saw it, his heart seemed to stop, but his hand snatched up a rock and hurled it with deadly accuracy.

Sierra screamed when he grabbed her hand and jerked her towards him. She struggled in his arms.

He held her and spun around, pointing toward the smashed reptile. "Now do you see why you need to leave here?"

With a violent shove, she pushed him away. "Stay away from me. I'll not leave here because I know in my heart that this is where God wants me. Do I make myself clear?"

His head shook in denial. "It's too late. You already love me, and I love you."

Those three little words seared her heart. She saw by his eyes he meant them. "Josh please, make peace with God."

He made a move toward her.

"No, don't touch me. If you love me, you'll keep your distance. I'm going back to the village now, and I want to go alone."

"Something's happened between them." Elizabeth McCabe whispered to her husband as they knelt by their bed for their prayer time. "They hardly spoke at dinner time, and their faces are a picture of misery."

"I noticed the strain between them Lizbeth," James said, and leaned an elbow on the patchwork quilt, giving his wife a shoulder hug. "It was first on my list for our prayer time. It's best just to turn it over to the Lord, and let him work it out."

"But I had my hopes up so high that she was sent in answer to our prayers."

James McCabe smiled at his wife. "She well may be Lizbeth. Give God time to work now. Don't rush him. Do you want to open our talk with the Lord or shall I?"

Chapter 15

"With Josh's extra help we've almost completed the landing strip, Lizbeth." James McCabe rinsed the dish that Elizabeth handed him and sat it in the drain-rack. "It's been wonderful to have him with us the last few weeks. But when he and Sierra are in the same room, the tension is thicker than the jungle."

Elizabeth nodded. "There's still a terrible strain between them. Even more since the drum messages began. All our prayers don't seem to be helping."

"Now, don't rush God, dear wife. His timetable's much different than ours. Be patient."

"But if anything, the rift between them has widened. I saw Josh trying to talk to her this morning, and she was obviously very upset with what he had to say. I pray that God will do something quickly before their relationship is beyond repair."

"Maybe a little breathing room is what they need. Why don't I ask him to come with me down to the station to pick up that part that finally came in?"

Elizabeth tilted her head to the side and then nodded. "That might be just the thing. After all, there must be some truth to the old saying about separation and the heart. It'll give Sierra and I some time to concentrate on the translation without distractions also. It's absolutely amazing how fast that girl's learning the language. She's improving daily."

"How dare he try to frighten me with such stories?" Sierra thought of Josh's warning about the drums and mumbled to herself while she took her daily walk through the village. She stopped to watch a native woman work, her grass skirt swaying gracefully. She was washing sago palm fibers to remove the starch, which was the bread of life to the natives. A baby lay on a soft bed of leaves, and an older child sat nearby keeping watch over her tiny sibling.

Sierra greeted them, politely inquiring about the children. The baby boy chortled and waved his arms with excitement as his older sister made playful noises to entertain him. The young woman complimented her skill as a baby sitter and was rewarded by a smile. With innocent curiosity, the little girl stared at Sierra from huge almond shaped eyes framed by exquisitely long lashes that rivaled those of any movie star.

"You're very beautiful. What's your name?" Sierra asked in their language.

With a shy smile, the girl replied, "Sariase."

Sierra tried the musical syllables on her tongue. "Sah-ree-ah-say. That's so pretty. It sounds like a bird singing." Without thought, she had switched back to English. Sariase tilted her head from side to side as she listened to Sierra's voice, and then she repeated the word singing. Realizing she had a willing student, Sierra repeated the words in both languages. The little girl smiled in understanding; and with excellent results for her first effort, she repeated the few words after Sierra.

Obviously proud of her offspring, Sariase's mother complimented her daughter on her success and thanked Sierra humbly for visiting with them. While she spoke the drums began again as they had everyday for over a week.

From her place by Sierra, Zephon raised her wings and lifted into the air trying to locate the source of the repetitive messages, but after the incident with the snake-disguised demon, she dared not go for from her charge.

Remembering Josh's warning, Sierra asked the woman if she knew the meaning of the rhythmic sound. Sariase's mother took so long to reply, she seemed not to have heard her, but after a lengthy pause, she lifted her head from her work, and her words sent a chill down Sierra's spine. Josh had spoken the truth. She thanked the woman automatically and then retraced her steps to the mission house followed by the now ominous sound of the drums.

Elizabeth McCabe took one look at Sierra's face and led her to a chair at the kitchen table. "Are you all right? You're whiter than my grandma's apron."

"The drums *are* talking about me." She sank into the chair and whispered the words.

"Yes dear, they're talking about you, but there's nothing unusual about that. The tribes have competed with each other for years to see who would have the white man come live with them. We're a source of many material blessings to them in addition to the spiritual blessing we bring."

"But Josh said they're talking about how I look, my hair and eyes."

Elizabeth laughed lightly, with a twinkle in her brown eyes. "They're simply bragging about how unusual their new foreigner is. They've never seen anyone who looks like you. For that matter dear, I've never seen anyone who looks like you. Your coloring is quite unique and beautiful."

Sierra managed a weak smile. "Thank you. You must think I'm being very silly."

Elizabeth shook her head. "Not at all dear. This culture's completely alien to us. It takes time to adjust. There are many things that are strange and frightening at first. You're doing remarkably well for your first time on the field. I'm sorry if my son said something that upset you."

At the mention of Josh, Sierra's face fell once again.

Elizabeth placed her hand comfortingly on her shoulder and sat down beside her. "I don't mean to pry dear, but you and my troubled son seem to have had a serious disagreement. Is there any way I can help?"

Concern and caring where written all over Elizabeth McCabe's face, and Sierra felt an urgent need to share her burden with a woman who was older and wiser. Not wanting to ruin the other woman's happiness, but feeling she must confide in someone, Sierra plunged ahead. "Josh asked me to leave here with him. He wants me to give up being a missionary. He says I'm motivated by guilt."

"Oh no. Things are much worse than I knew. Why would he think that's your motivation?" Elizabeth said.

Sierra hung her head. "Because my parents were scheduled to work in Irian Jaya as Bible translators, and it's my fault they and my aunt and uncle died." She raised her hand when Elizabeth started to interrupt. "Wait. Josh is right. I was lost, but it wasn't an accident. I saw the sign and the barrier, but the powder looked so inviting, and I planned to only go a short way." She lifted her head, but she couldn't meet Elizabeth's eyes. "The worst part is Ellie's parents were not Christians, and I don't know if they had time to talk to God before they died." Her hands twisted together on the table.

Elizabeth covered them with hers. "Before your aunt and uncle died, did you ever pray for their salvation?"

Sierra nodded her head vigorously. "Yes, my parents and I always prayed for them."

"Then you can be assured that they had time. It is not God's will that anyone be lost." Elizabeth's grip tightened on her hand. "You told my son no, of course."

Sierra nodded solemnly, and her eyes filled with tears. "I can't leave here."

"Good for you dear," Elizabeth said and smiled, patting Sierra's hand. "Stick to your guns. I'm sorry this is so painful for you."

"I'm so confused. Forgive me, but sometimes I wish Josh would leave, so I can continue my work in peace. There's a wall of solid rock between his heart and God. I keep praying that he'll let go of the pain and anger; but if anything, it seems to be getting worse. There's an urgency about him, like a volcano that's getting ready to explode." As she released her troubled thoughts, Sierra's words came faster and faster, like clouds driven by the wind before a storm.

"James was right. You and Josh need to be apart for awhile. I think you'll be relieved to hear that James is going to ask Josh to make a trip to the mission station with him. They'll be gone three days. That should give you a chance to catch your breath."

"Thank you Elizabeth. I'm sorry I burdened you with all of that."

"There's nothing to be sorry for dear. I'm glad I was able to help. I hope you'll always come to me when you feel the need to talk. It makes troubles seem a lot lighter when you have someone to share them with. Please come to me anytime." She stood up and moved to the coffee bar.

"Thank you. I will. That's one thing I've missed since I left Texas. My grandmother was always there for me when I needed to seek sage advice. I miss her more than I thought possible."

Elizabeth looked back at her as she poured coffee for herself. "Would you like some?" At Sierra's nod, she filled a second cup and returned to her seat. "Separation from family and close friends is one of the hardest parts of this work. Being isolated from their loving support is more difficult than one can imagine. You were very close to your grandmother?"

"Yes, she raised my cousin Eleanor and me. We were orphaned at a very young age."

"Oh. Is this the same cousin at whose party you met my son?"

"Yes. Ellie's always been a little wild. She was always talking me into mischief when we were kids. I remember one summer we were playing on the hill behind grandmother's house. Ellie talked me into riding with her down the hill in our red wagon. She made it sound like it would be great fun. And it was, until we realized we had no way to stop, and we were headed straight for the river at the bottom of the hill."

From her position beside Briel, just outside the kitchen door, Zephon's ears tuned into the conversation because she clearly remembered the incident. It happened shortly after she became Sierra's guardian.

"Oh my, what happened?" Elizabeth leaned forward.

"When I saw the danger we were in I closed my eyes and started praying as hard as I could," Sierra continued, "What happened next is so clearly impressed in my memory, it's like it happened only yesterday. I heard Ellie scream and then a splash as the wagon hit the water, and then I felt as though a giant hand reached out and pressed us down into the mud on the river bottom. It was amazing. Our momentum and the buoyancy of the wagon should have carried us out into the current where we would surely have drowned. I climbed out of that wagon and waded to dry land, feeling thankful to be alive. I remembered a verse that grandmother had taught me—'The angel of the Lord encamps all around those who fear him and delivers them'. That verse jumped into my mind, and I knew God was taking care of me."

Briel noticed Zephon's rapt attention to the story. "You were there?"

"Yes." Zephon nodded.

"Well done," Briel said, and saluted her with a bow.

Zephon lifted her wings in a shrug. "Just doing my job, and Sierra's prayer made it easier."

Elizabeth's face glowed as she felt the power of God's presence in the young girl's life. "I believe God brought that childhood memory back to your mind just now for a reason. He wants to remind you that he's always taking care of you, even in these present difficult circumstances, and he also wants to remind you that he answers prayer, like the prayers for your aunt and uncle."

At her friend's words, peace like a warm blanket on a cold night wrapped around Sierra. She breathed out a sigh of relief when she realized the truth in Elizabeth's words. "Maybe he's also reminding me of the importance of fervent prayer. That was the first time I prayed really hard, and I truly learned its value."

Zephon nodded. "Yes. It strengthened my arm and gave me the power to save you."

"Thank you so much for listening, Elizabeth. Would you pray with me about Josh?"

"I'd love to." She gave Sierra a hug and they bowed their heads and hearts together.

Chapter 16

"Josh and I may need to postpone our trip to the mission station if the weather doesn't clear," James McCabe said, donning his pajamas, and looked out the bedroom window, "Lord willing, this storm will have blown itself out by morning."

The storm showed no signs of abating. Another howl roared around the house as the wind attacked the building, driving the rain before it with brutal force. The weather had changed rapidly; dawn broke bright and clear the morning after Sierra and Elizabeth had their heart to heart talk, but it changed to torrential rain by mid-afternoon.

"I hope none of the natives are out in this," Elizabeth said, her brow creasing. "Many of them went to a neighboring village this morning. Do you think they would try to come back in this storm?"

"Now Lizbeth, I'm sure there's no cause for worry. The natives know how to deal with this kind of weather. I'm sure they'll wait tell it's safe."

"I do hope so. The village is on the other side of the river. You know how it treacherous it can be when swollen from the rain."

Sierra had tossed and turned for hours, unable to sleep even after the storm had eased off because occasional gusts of wind rattled the windows loudly causing her to awaken just when slumber was about to claim her. Finally, calm seemed to be returning as the wind abated, and she felt her mind slipping into a state of rest in the blessed quiet.

A loud pounding on the front door of the mission house and the frantic voice of a native in severe distress startled Sierra into instant alertness. She jumped from her bed. Throwing on her clothing, she heard the reassuring tones of James McCabe advising the late caller of their wakefulness, then she rushed from her room and hurried to join the others at the front of the house.

A frightened native was speaking so rapidly she had trouble understanding him. With wild gestures and a rush of words he seemed to be telling them of an accident on the river.

In a calm voice James McCabe quieted the agitated man and after asking him several pertinent questions, had assessed the situation. "The natives tried to cross the river after the rain stopped, thinking they could do so by forming a human chain." He spoke rapidly, explaining to Sierra while he gathered flashlights and extra batteries. "The men carry a heavy rock or their woman or child on their shoulders. The extra weight and the chain of people holding hands helps them wade across without being washed away by the force of the water. It usually works, but this time an unexpected wall of water washed them all downstream."

"Oh no!" Elizabeth and Sierra gasped.

"We need to hurry." James headed out the door followed closely by his wife, the native messenger, Sierra, and Josh. The native moved ahead of them and led the way at a fast pace toward the river.

The angels encircled the group and kept a wary eye out for the enemy, who frequently used the darkness as their ally.

James continued as they neared the riverbank. "Everyone made it to shore only to discover the child Sariase was missing from the sarong on her mother's back. They've searched for her; but without light and with the moon obscured by the clouds most of the time, they've been unable to locate her."

"We need to pray." Sierra reached for Elizabeth's hand as she spoke.

"You're absolutely right. Let's stop right this minute and do so." Elizabeth agreed. Matching deeds to words, she reached for her husband's hand and pulled him to a halt.

"Son, would you join us?" James McCabe extended his hand to Josh and waited hopefully.

Josh joined hands with the small group, but he looked toward the river, thinking their time would be better spent looking for the lost child, but unable to voice his doubts to his parents.

"Father in heaven," Sierra spoke with urgency, "this precious child is in severe danger. Please do a miracle, Lord, and save her." She waited, and the two older missionaries added their entreaties for the child's safety.

Hovering above the group with their swords in hand, the angels spread their wings wide, and their swords begin to shimmer. The light spread, turning the blades to flame.

A pregnant silence followed, as though the three prayers all held their breath expecting Josh to pray also. Josh gritted his teeth, resisting the desire to join his voice with theirs and wondering if he even remembered how. He realized that he hadn't prayed for a very long time, even before Michael and Sarah died. Like air into a vacuum, he felt himself pulled to respond. Memories rushed at him, a kaleidoscope of scenes of bowed heads and open hearts, but two beloved faces were missing from the circle on the riverbank.

James McCabe spoke into the silence, "Father, show your power to these natives, and to everyone who doubts you, by saving this child's life. In Jesus' precious name, amen."

Many of the villagers still roamed the banks of the river, calling the child's name, but others had retreated to their warm dry huts, sure the rushing water had drowned the small girl.

With flashlights on high beam the new rescue party began to search.

Sierra looked at the normally pleasant river, amazed to find it a mass of churning brown water, and she wondered if a small child could survive. *Only with your help, Lord. Please, don't let little Sariase, the little girl who's name sounds like a bird singing, be gone, Father. Save her.* Sierra continued to pray while she searched, calling the child's name, and suddenly a sound no louder than a whimper caught her ear; it seemed to be coming from the middle of the river. She swung the beam of light quickly over the water, looking intently for the small form of a little girl. Stopping the forward motion of her hand, she brought the light back to a solid mass in the middle of the rushing water. Yes! There was definitely something there. A sandbar or a cluster of branches, or something that resisted the force of the water, and a sound of distress came from the area. "Here! Come quickly! I think I've found her!"

Her call brought the others running to gather round her, looking to the spot where she pointed. "There, see. There's something solid in the middle of the river. And I thought I heard a child's cry. She's there. I know it. Listen!" The faint but distinct cry came again, sending a ripple of excitement through the group.

Without any preamble, Josh took charge. "We'll form a chain of men. I'll lead the way. I'm the largest, heaviest person here, so the water won't be able to carry me downstream." He grabbed the hand of the native next to him. All of the men followed suit, and the line moved into the water with Josh in the lead.

Raphael and Arioch winged their way over the human chain, their swords ready to prevent the enemies interference.

Sierra and Elizabeth joined hands, praying fervently while they shone the flashlights over the water, making a trail of light from the shore to the small island of life in the middle of the river.

The child's cries grew stronger when she realized help was on the way. The sound was sweeter than laughter to the ears of all those who struggled to reach her.

Sierra's eyes locked on the form of the man in the lead. He fought to remain standing in the violent current, then suddenly he disappeared from sight, going under the raging water. "No!" A cry of denial tore from her lips when she saw him go down.

Like a hawk attacking his prey, Raphael dove into the water, slashing at the demon that pushed Josh's feet from their precarious perch on the river's uneven bed. The demon fought back; drawing his own blade, he struggled to hold Josh down and ward off the attacker. But the demon was no match for the angel's empowered arm; Raphael drove the enemy from the water with his sword, grabbed

Josh by the arm and, with a quick thrust, propelled Josh toward the surface.

Sierra leaned toward the water, his name like a prayer on her lips. A sigh of relief escaped her as he re-surfaced, and she realized she had been holding her breath.

Josh wiped the muddy water from his eyes, looked around him to find the person who helped him to the surface, and saw no one within reach. The water's swift current had carried him from the group. The natives and his father were still in line. He shook his head, and forced himself to look for a path through the torrent. Only a few feet separated him from the little girl who clung tenaciously to a pile of branches wedged against a clump of rock in the middle of the river. He knew that time was their enemy; at any moment another wave of water could come hurling down from the mountaintop to wash the small girl from her perch. Placing his feet carefully, he worked his way through the water. A cheer went up from the watchers when he reached the little girl, and lifted her into his arms. He sat her on his wide shoulders with instructions to hold tight, and then he began the return trip.

Tears of joy ran down the face of Sariase's mother when Josh placed the child safely in her arms.

"Thank you God." Elizabeth McCabe and her husband said in unison and then hugged each other, laughing in relief.

Sierra's feet carried her to stand beside Josh. "That was the bravest thing I've ever seen anyone do. You were wonderful," Sierra whispered as they watched the happy reunion of the native family.

The unexpected praise was balm to his aching heart, and he turned to look at her. The moon shone from a break in the clouds causing the tears on her cheeks to sparkle like dewdrops in the sun. His hand moved to touch her face, and he gently wiped the tears away, his fingers caressing her skin. "It was nothing, really."

Sierra shivered and crossed her arms. "It was much more than nothing. God did a miracle, and you were part of it," she replied with quiet conviction.

A curtain seemed to come down over his face at her words. "Call it that if you must." Without a backward glance he set a rapid pace for the mission house, trying to put from his mind the memory of the hand that thrust him from the water.

"It's absolutely amazing," Elizabeth said in wonder, while she repacked her first aid cabinet, "every single adult involved in the accident has cuts and scrapes from the rocks in the river. I have treated several dozen people today, but the child doesn't have a mark on her."

James McCabe chuckled. "If you think that's amazing, you should hear what's being said in the village. The story's being told over and over again about how the God of the foreigner's saved the child because we asked Him to. The people are saying the God we worship is very strong if he can defeat the river demons. The miracle's continuing Lizbeth. God's using this to open the natives' hearts."

"Oh James, that's so wonderful. If only God would use it to open our son's heart also. Did you hear what he said to Sierra last night after the rescue?"

"I heard. Josh has always been strong willed and stubborn. I don't know what it's going to take to bring him round."

Chapter 17

"We should be back in three days, Lizbeth." James McCabe continued loading his backpack as he spoke, arranging the neatly folded clothing and the packages of food with care. "Lord willing, and the weather cooperates. Do you remember how to use the ham radio?"

"Yes, I believe so James. Don't you worry about Sierra and I. We'll be fine. We have plenty to keep us busy. Some of the native women have begun asking questions about God, and we plan to take full advantage of the open door. We're to have our first Bible study using the Gospel of John. I'm so excited James."

"Well, I can see you'll be too busy to even miss me." He commented and smiled at her. "I hope our son is ready to go. I had a difficult task in convincing him to go with me. He made a lot of excuses but never mentioned the true reason. I believe he simply doesn't want to leave Sierra."

"She and I had a long talk the day before the accident on the river. She was very distraught because they had an argument."

"They seem to have a lot of those."

"This time was more serious. Josh told her he loves her."

"And that upset her?" James interjected.

"Let me finish, dear. That was only part of it. He also asked Sierra to give up her work here and come away with him."

James McCabe moved his head in denial and put a hand to his

forehead. "I'm afraid our son's hardened heart is much worse than I thought." Then another thought occurred to him. "She turned him down, of course."

"Yes. But I could tell it was very hard for her. I encouraged her to stand firm and resist the temptation. She said she would but I think it's another matter for prayer. Our son can be very persuasive."

Her husband's face fell into deep lines of concern while he pondered this information. "It's good that they'll be apart for a few days. It sounds like she needs some time to solidify her resolve."

Zephon watched her charge pace back and forth in her room. Raphael had warned her to be even more vigilant while he and Arioch were away with Josh and his father. She saw the struggle within Sierra, but no demons were involved.

Sierra debated for the tenth time whether she should go out to say good-bye to Josh and his father as they left for the mission station. "I know he was reluctant to go with his father, and I think it's because of me. If I go out there, will it make him change his mind? Should I stay in my room?" She stopped speaking to herself, but her mind still wrestled at full speed.

A soft gentle voice entered into the chaos of her thoughts. *Pray Sierra, ask for guidance.* "Father in heaven, what should I do?" In her mind, she saw herself going out, and she knew she had her answer.

Josh snapped together the last buckle on his backpack and looked up when she entered the front room. Their eyes met and held. She walked toward him, stopping only a few feet away. He fought the desire to insist that she come with him, leaving Irian Jaya and missionary work behind.

Sierra closed her eyes to break the contact that seemed to be pulling her toward Josh with an inexorable force. *Help me to be strong, Lord.* "I hope you'll have a safe trip." The steadiness of her words surprised her because she felt herself trembling inwardly.

"You take care while I'm gone, promise." Real concern colored his words, making them sound like a demand for reassurance.

"I will, I promise."

"Stay close to the village. Don't go wandering around by yourself."

A little pinprick of fear touched her. "Are you trying to frighten me?"

"No. I'm trying to warn you. Just do as I say."

"You're really worried, aren't you?"

His jaw tightened at her words, making it's square lines look rock solid. "I have a bad feeling about this. That's all."

"It's the story about the Kai, isn't it?" She crossed her arms and gave him a triumphant smile. "You're finally beginning to believe that the lady of the legend is me."

"Don't look so smug. You forget I grew up here on this island. There's sometimes a lot of truth in their legends. But whether it's true or not, the question is, do the natives believe it? If they do, it's frightening to contemplate what might happen. I've never heard the drums talk like they've talked since you came here. I don't like the sound of it."

Sierra's resolve to keep her distance from Josh vanished like mist in the wind. Unaware of her own movement she took a step towards him and laid her hand on his arm. "It'll be all right Josh. You'll see."

A current leaped from her body to his and back again, pulling them together, its power growing stronger with each passing second. She leaned towards him.

"Your father's ready to go Josh." Elizabeth McCabe's voice preceded her before she came into the room.

Sierra jumped in alarm. Her heart pounded louder than the drums, and she realized her willpower was much weaker than she thought when it came to resisting her attraction to Josh.

From their position just outside the dwelling, Zephon and Briel watched the native women walk toward the mission house. "I sense no danger from them," Briel said, and turned her dark eyes toward Zephon just as the ever-present drums increased their tempo.

"I agree," Zephon replied. "But why do you suppose the drum

rhythm grew more intense just now? I don't like it. The enemy's moving somewhere."

"They shall not interfere with the work of our ladies today," Briel said, and touched her sword.

"Look Elizabeth," Sierra commented as she glanced out the window when the time drew near for the ladies Bible study, "isn't that Sariase's mother?"

"Yes. Her name is Sirowi, and I believe the young woman with her is her sister Kani. The older woman is her mother Imati. The child's rescue seems to have made a great impression on them. Let's pray quickly that God would empower us in a special way to reach these ladies for him."

They bowed their heads together; and as Elizabeth prayed, Sierra felt the presence and power of the Lord enter the room. She knew Elizabeth felt it also, because when she finished praying, she lifted her head with a radiant smile.

"We're in His perfect will, Sierra," Elizabeth said. She squeezed the young woman's hands and then turned to greet their guests. Elizabeth made introductions and then invited everyone to be seated.

The native women looked with great curiosity at the contents of the foreigner's house, so different from their own. The furnishings were Spartan and barely adequate by western standards but seemed wondrously luxurious to the primitive tribeswomen. Elizabeth gave them time to look, realizing she needed to let them get acclimated somewhat before beginning. Speaking with care in their language, she inquired about their children, encouraging them to talk. The familiar subject allowed the woman to relax in the strange surroundings and become more comfortable.

Sierra was happy to discover that she understood most of what was said. Her grasp of their language was almost one hundred percent now.

Feeling that the timing was right, Elizabeth picked up the computer printout of the Gospel of John. "As my husband and I explained to your people when we first came to you, Jehovah, who is the one true God, commanded everyone who believes in him to go to all peoples everywhere in the world and tell them about him. Since we came to you, we've learned your language, and we've began putting God's word into your language. We've now finished part of the word of God in your language. This," Elizabeth said, lifting the computer printout from her lap and holding it before her, "is that finished part."

The native women leaned forward, looking at the white pages with the many small black marks. They knew Kito, one of the village men, had been working with the foreigners on this, and they were curious to hear more about it.

Elizabeth continued. "I'd like to read some of it to you, and then we can talk about it. Please feel free to ask any questions. Sierra and I will try our best to answer them. In time, we'll teach you how to read the word of God for yourself, if you wish to learn."

The island women all nodded their heads vigorously. They listened with rapt attention while Elizabeth lifted the pages and began to read.

"In the beginning was the word, and the word was with God, and the word was God. He was with God in the beginning. Through him all things were made; without him nothing was made that has been made. In him was life, and that life was the light of men. The light shines in the darkness, but the darkness has not understood it..." Elizabeth continued.

Sirowi, Kani, and Imati had listened to the stories their men brought back from the manhouse. Kito took great pleasure in being the center of attention there. He daily revealed the wonders he learned about at the foreigner's house. But the second hand information had not prepared them for the power they heard in these words.

Elizabeth stopped when she completed the first chapter. As if on cue, all three of the avid listeners broke into excited speech. With a laugh, she held up her hand and tried to restore order. It was all she could do to answer one question before another was fired at her.

Sierra watched and listened in awe, amazed at how quickly the women applied God's word to their lives. Seeing that Elizabeth was swamped in questions, she breathed a quick prayer for assistance and entered the conversation. With reverent care, she attempted to introduce her new friends to the love of God.

CHAPTER 18

"Only one and one-half days since they left. I wonder if they're headed back yet." Sierra mumbled to herself as she walked through the village. She passed the trail to the forest pool, and her steps slowed. "Josh was right. I was motivated by guilt for what happened to Ellie's parents." She put a hand to the neckline of her blue camp shirt and swallowed. Since her conversation with Elizabeth about Josh's accusation, the load of guilt had lightened. "Did they have time to talk to you Father?" She closed her eyes and prayed with all her heart that they did, and her heart lifted.

Zephon walked beside her, sword in hand, ever mindful of the enemy's strength in the area. With relief, she noted that the drums failed to sound at their usual time.

Sierra shook her head against her troubled thoughts and tried to focus on her surroundings. All around her the native woman went about their daily activities; their lives centered on the care of their children and the gathering and preparation of food. They smiled with shyness and returned Sierra's greetings as she spoke first to one and then another. Arriving at the far edge of the large cluster of huts, she was about to turn and retrace her steps when a chorus of jubilant shouting reached her ears. The women stopped their work and ran toward the sound, and their voices echoed in cheers of praise. Their men had returned triumphant from a wild boar hunt.

The hunters danced in wild abandon when they entered the

clearing. At their center, on a pole carried by the two men who had delivered the killing blows, hung the massive wild pig. Its horn-trimmed snout dripped blood. The women exclaimed at the size of the pig, proclaiming it to be the largest ever killed by anyone in their village, and the grandfather of all pigs. The hunters beamed at the adulation, pounded their chests and strutted proudly.

Sierra watched in fascination while they made the pig ready for the spit. The natives talked with excitement while they worked, and she gathered from their conversation that such a prize was an occasion for a great celebration, and the whole village would join in. When the pig was ready for cooking, a young boy was given the honor of turning the spit while the pig slowly roasted. The women gathered in small groups to prepare the side dishes, while the men entertained them all by recounting in minute detail every moment of the hunt. The aromas of exotic foods began to fill the air, dominated by the mouth-watering smell of barbecued pork.

Glancing toward the mission house Sierra saw Elizabeth standing on the porch observing the festivities with a smile. The young woman waved at her coworker and received a raised hand in reply.

A group of dancing children asked Sierra to join them as they copied their elders in a dance of victory. Laughing at her awkwardness, she tried to follow the intricate foot patterns while they chanted a rhythm.

The afternoon waned, and the celebration continued. Hungry natives crowded round the roasted boar, its tender flesh seasoned to perfection by the smoke produced from the dripping juices, and consumed it with great pleasure. Sariase brought Sierra a platter of food, smiling in delight at the young woman's abundant thanks.

The shadows grew long. Sierra began to notice the pairing off of couples, and a feeling of isolation and aloneness settled over her. Thanking her friends for including her in their celebration, she left the village and headed toward the mission house. She came abreast of the path to the orchid pool, and her feet turned down the path.

Zephon frowned at Sierra's change of direction but followed dutifully. The continued silence of the drums made her less wary than previously.

Sierra followed the worn footpath, watching her step and keeping her eyes alert for the crossing trees landmark. After what seemed a much longer span of time than her walk with Josh, she had almost decided to backtrack, thinking she must have missed the landmark while watching her footing. She stopped, looking around for a familiar sight. The large tree fern ahead on the trail struck a chord in her memory. She proceeded past the feathery fronds and looked around her once more.

"There! That's it." She spotted the giant crossed trees. "The path must be around here somewhere." Lining up with the giant X of the crossed palms to the best of her memory, she looked down at the jungle floor. "Yes!" The narrow, barely discernible, path was there. She stepped onto it and pushed her way through the thick jungle foliage. Keeping the landmark X in her sight, she followed the thin trail and emerged into the clearing with a sigh of pleasure. "It's just as beautiful as I remembered."

She pushed the memory of the dead snake from her mind when the natural rock bench beckoned her, and she made herself comfortable, listening to the birdsong while she drank in the serenity of the place. The peaceful spot lulled her senses, and she closed her eyes, breathing deeply the fragrance of the orchids.

Mindful of the demon attack in that spot, Zephon's alertness level went into high gear. Her senses buzzed, and her sword vibrated in warning. With a thrust of her wings, she lifted into the air over Sierra's head to better survey the scene. *I think we're in trouble Sierra; you better pray. And I hope lots of other people are praying too.*

The scene with Josh replayed itself in Sierra's mind. Every vivid detail had been captured by her memory and now invoked a bittersweet response. She bowed her head and began to pray. "Father in heaven, what am I going to do? I love him, and I'm fast losing the will to fight the attraction I feel for him. Please change his heart. Bring him back to you." Remembering Josh's accusation that her missionary calling was prompted by guilt, she added. "Help me to serve you with a guilt free heart. Your will be done Father. I love you. In Jesus' name, amen." She had whispered the prayer softly but with fervent passion.

As her prayer ceased, she felt an eerie stillness in the tiny jungle glade; every bird had fallen silent leaving only the whispering of the trees in the wind. Something ominous had invaded the small clearing. Suddenly aware of her isolation from the village, warnings of jungle dangers raced through her mind. Afraid of what she would find, but knowing she must, Sierra opened her eyes, and her breath stopped. Her hands flew to her heart as it slammed against her ribs.

Warriors completely surrounded her. Death masks of black and white paint covered their faces, and their nearly naked bodies wore little more than bones and feathers. A clammy chill raised the flesh on her arms when she noticed the grizzly remains of their hunts hanging from the shaft of their spears—shrunken heads, the empty eye sockets staring vacantly into space, dangled in clusters from the primitive weapons.

A scream tried to erupt from her throat, but she choked it down; caution warned her that kind of reaction could be instantly fatal. At any rate, the chance of her screams reaching someone's ears over the noisy festivities in the village seemed unlikely because the sheer density of the jungle itself absorbed and muted sounds.

Zephon's eyes scanned the crowd of native warriors, sensing the presence of the enemy. *There, in the back.* She spotted a large group of demons with their talons attached to the body of an older native who wore a skull headdress. *The witchdoctor, no doubt.* She felt the power of many prayers for Sierra's safety, but she knew she was outnumbered and couldn't risk a defeat, which would leave Sierra exposed to extreme danger. Strategy, not raw power, must rule the day. She noted that most of the natives were demon free and might be used as allies. *If there's enough prayer? Pray Sierra, pray.* Casting off her invisibility, Zephon spread her wings wide and raised her fiery sword.

An "ah" of amazement went up from the natives, and at almost the same moment, from the back of the group, Sierra heard a roar of anger and a hideous apparition surged toward her. The other natives heard it also, and turned in force with their spears raised.

Seeing her opportunity, Zephon vanished and flew at the demons, slashing in righteous anger at their blackened skin. They screamed and writhed under her blade, and most of them scurried away, dragging their wounded limbs behind them, but one stood to fight. Bigger and more powerful than the rest, he raised a bloodstained sword and beckoned to her with a blackened claw.

"Come, little angel," the demon said, and leered. "If you dare."

"Pray Sierra, pray," Zephon implored her charge. "I've never fought such a powerful demon before, but it's not the power of my arm that matters, it's the power of your prayers."

The witchdoctor advanced toward Sierra, staff raised to strike. He plowed through the native warriors, oblivious to their blows.

"Father in heaven, I'm frightened. Help me," Sierra whispered skyward and shivered. She tried to run, but her legs refused to move.

Like an avenging wind, Zephon whirled around the demon, her blade thrusting with a tormenting fire. He twisted and turned, chopping ineffectually at her, and then she saw an opening and delivered a crippling blow. The demon howled in rage, tore himself from the witch doctor's body, and vanished in a trail of black vapor. Zephon watched the witch doctor run from the clearing and disappear into the jungle. *I have a feeling we haven't seen the last of either of those two.*

Sierra had watched the natives attack one of their own and wondered. "Are they protecting me, Lord?"

I am with you always, even until the end of the age. A sweet gentle voice sounded clearly in her mind; it brought a feeling of peace and submission to God's will. *Do you love me Sierra?*

"Yes, Lord. You know that I love you."

Than feed my sheep and love them Sierra. Perfect love casts out fear. She heard the voice in her mind again.

To her utter amazement, one by one the native warriors turned towards her and began to kneel before her and bow their heads to the ground. Recognizing with horror that they were worshiping her, Sierra cried out, "No!"

At her cry, the natives raised their heads. Vigorously shaking her head, hoping to communicate she was no god to be worshipped, she motioned for them to rise. Speaking to them in the local language resulted in blank stares of incomprehension.

A warrior in an intricate headdress of feathers and bones stepped forward. With fluid hands, he indicated Sierra should follow him. At her negative head motion, he gave what could only be a command to the surrounding natives. They all stepped forward, tightening the circle around Sierra, leaving no doubt in her mind they intended for her to accompany them, willing or not.

I can't go with them! No! Father, help me, please. I can't do this! Did you lead me to Irian only to have me captured by headhunters? Can this be your will? All the calm reassurance Sierra felt only a few moments before completely deserted her. She shivered. Beads of moisture gathered on her brow. Her legs almost buckled. *Lord, please make this go away. I was wrong to come here. Help me.*

The leader stepped toward Sierra, repeating his hand signal; his dark eyes waited expectantly for her response.

Scenes from the last few weeks flew through her mind like a movie on fast forward and came to a screeching halt with Josh's warning. She closed her eyes and hung her head as remorse overwhelmed her. *I'm so foolish and arrogant. Please forgive me for my know-it-all attitude of superiority. What should I do Lord?* With mounting trepidation she waited, hoping God would do a miracle.

Go unto the ends of the earth. The voice was fainter now, but she knew that she had her answer. With a reluctant nod to the head warrior, she gave her assent; and then, on shaky legs, followed as the warrior led the way through the jungle.

The natives set a fast pace, leaving the high valley that nestled in the foothills of the interior, to head directly for the towering mountains.

Where are they taking me? Maybe I should make a run for it. No, no. She shook her head at the thought, realizing she would be no match for her captors. They were at home in this wild environment, while she would be hopelessly lost within minutes. *Besides, God just told me to go unto the ends of the earth. But not like this! As a captive!* Fear made her legs stiff, but it also forced her to keep on walking or face the natives' retaliation.

Zephon flew high above the trees, in an effort to locate the witch doctor and the powerful demon who challenged her, but she kept an eye on her charge at all times. She detected no sign of the enemy or his human arm, but she knew they were out there somewhere, hiding in the jungle. *Where are these natives taking Sierra? And what are their plans for her?*

The jungle-choked mountains seemed impenetrable to Sierra, but the natives threaded their way. Branches slapped her face, and vines tangled in her hair, but her captors stopped for nothing. They climbed vigorously and showed no signs of slowing their pace, even though the evening shadows darkened. The stars begin to come out, and the moon rose over the mountains, a huge golden ball in the sky.

She struggled to keep up with them, her thoughts a chaotic jumble. Glancing at her watch, Sierra saw they had been walking for hours. *Will Elizabeth notice my absence? Or will she believe I'm still at the celebration in the village? When will Josh and his father return? Will they be able to follow our trail? Will these natives release me even if Josh and his father find us? Or will they kill me and anyone who attempts a rescue. Where are these headhunters taking me? Judging by their behavior in the glade, they have some sort of reverence for me. Do they eat people they revere?* She shuddered at the thought and her heart felt as if it would be torn in two by the fear. *Father in heaven, have I come all the way to Irian Jaya only to be killed?*

The serene assurance came again. *For I know the plans I have for you, plans for good and not for evil, to give you a future and a hope.* Holding onto that promise like a drowning man to his last breath of air, Sierra continued to follow her captors higher into the mountain wilderness.

The hills became steeper, and her legs burned. Breathing was difficult, as the air grew thinner in the high altitude, and after negotiating a particularly difficult slope, she stopped, bent over, and placed her hands on her knees. Gasping for breath, she made another attempt at the local dialect. "I have to rest. I'm not used to the lack of oxygen. I know you don't understand a word I'm saying, but you must see I can't continue at this pace."

The native leader trotted back down the trail to stop at her side. He seemed to assess his captive and come to a decision. After several sharp commands from him, his warriors melted into the jungle, leaving Sierra to wonder what was happening now. Her captor indicated she should sit, and she gladly sank onto a moss-covered rock, stretched aching legs in front of her, and waited to see what their plans would hold.

Zephon stayed close by the side of her charge now that they had stopped. She felt somewhat confident that Sierra was in no danger from the warrior leader and his band, judging by their treatment of her so far, but the demon-driven witch doctor might reappear at any time.

A warbling call much like the sound of a jungle bird echoed through the trees. With a spoken command that Sierra was beginning to understand to mean come, the warrior leader set off in the direction of the birdcall.

She thought it must have been a signal, and in spite of her fear, she was intrigued by their system of communication, but she had no time to analyze it further. Just moving required all her energy. Forcing her weary legs to support her, she followed close behind the leader.

The cave he led her to was small but warm and dry, and Sierra collapsed gratefully onto the sandy floor. Leaning against the solid rock wall, she rested her arms on her up-drawn knees. Through a haze of exhaustion she saw in her minds eye a face with hauntingly sad green eyes and a wealth of dark wavy hair. "Oh Josh, why didn't I heed your warning?" The tragic stories from his past echoed in her mind. "Oh no, what have I done to you?" She rested her head on her up-drawn knees and quietly gave in to the tears that had threatened for hours.

The cave walls looked shadowy in the flickering light from a fire when Sierra raised her head, and she realized that she must have fallen asleep. The smell of cooking meat reached her senses causing her stomach to growl. Through sleep blurry eyes she saw a young warrior remove from the cooking spit what appeared to be a small animal. Laying it on a large green leaf, he knelt before her, presenting it for her inspection. "I have no idea what it is, but it smells wonderful." She looked from the meat to the young native. "Is it for me to eat?" As if understanding her question, he lifted the offering toward her. She took the leaf plate from his outstretched hands, and said, "Thank you."

Sierra bowed her head over the jungle food. "Father in heaven, please bless this to my body and restore my strength. Thank you that you are working out this situation according to your perfect plan and for your glory. And Father, please help the McCabe family to know that I'm all right."

Sierra lifted her head to find over a dozen pairs of dark eyes starring at her with great curiosity. She realized they were wondering what she was doing with her head bowed over her food. Her love of language and her need to communicate with her captors replaced the tiredness and some of her remaining fear. She touched her chest with a flattened hand in the universal sign and said, "Sierra."

Chapter 19

The leader of the band of men came forward, squatted on his haunches close to her, and repeated her gesture on himself, saying, "Tohnii," and nodding his head.

Elated that he had grasped the word exchange so quickly, Sierra repeated his name, "Toe ne I," then she pointed to the fire and said the English word. He repeated her word and spoke a word in his language. She tried the new word on her tongue. He laughed and shook his head, repeating the word again, and she realized her intonation had been incorrect and tried again. This time he nodded his head in agreement. The lessons continued. She learned the name of every object she could find in their sparse surroundings until none remained, then to reinforce her memory she repeated them all again, and again. Tohnii patiently corrected her pronunciations and nodded his head with enthusiasm when she needed no help. The events of the day began to take their toll. She yawned repeatedly.

Seeing her tiredness, he issued an order whereupon several of his men left the cave to return in a few moments, their arms full of fluffy dry moss. They piled the moss by her, and she wondered if this was to be her bedding. The young warrior who had prepared the food began to spread out the spongy mass, taking great care to remove any sharp twigs as he worked. Satisfied with his work he indicated she should sleep now. Only to glad to comply, she lay down, almost asleep before her head touched the moss pillow.

Elizabeth McCabe awoke with a start. The early morning sun streamed in the windows, and the jungle birds screamed their raucous welcome to the new day. She stretched to ease the stiffness, and then laughed at herself for falling asleep on the rattan sofa while reading. She bathed and dressed for the day in a khaki blouse and culottes. "I wonder if Sierra would like some more pancakes for breakfast? She certainly is sleeping late this morning. I haven't heard a peep out of her." Knocking on her co-worker's door, she asked softly, "Are you awake dear?" Silence greeted her inquiry, and she frowned, tilting her head in perplexity. "Sierra, are you okay?" A niggling fear caused her to open the door and peer in. She found an empty room. Thinking Sierra must be there, she searched the room and then the entire mission house, hoping the young woman had risen early and was there somewhere.

Finding no sign of her, a cold dread settled over Elizabeth until another thought occurred to her. "Maybe she went to the village early. That's it, she's simply gone down to the village earlier than usual." Certain this was true, she left the mission house in a hurry.

After asking first one native and then another, her ominous foreboding returned and encased her heart in ice. All the natives told her the same story. The last time they saw the young missionary she was going back up the hill to the mission house. By all their estimates, that was yesterday, in the late afternoon.

"Dear Lord, where is she? Please don't let anything bad have happened to her. Keep her safe Lord. I implore you."

Hurrying back to the mission house, she almost ran to the study where the short wave radio was located. Her hands trembled when she lifted the microphone. "Foothills Mission House to Black Hills Mission Station, come in. This is an emergency! Come in. Cheryl, Pete, are you there? Over!"

The line crackled and buzzed with static, and Elizabeth thought she would need to repeat her call. Her hand reached for the microphone button and than paused in midair when she heard a welcome response.

"Black Hills Mission Station to Foothills Mission House, we copy your message. This is Pete. Are you all right Elizabeth? Over."

"Pete, thank God you're there! Are James and Josh there? Over."

"Negative, Elizabeth. They left this morning at sunrise. Your son was in a all-fired hurry to get back to someone up there. What's wrong? Over."

"Pete, Sierra's disappeared! I've looked everywhere for her. She's not in the house and she's not in the village. She's nowhere to be found! I don't know what to do! Over." Elizabeth's voice rose.

There was a stunned silence at the other end of the radio wave communication. Then a forcefully calm voice came over the airwaves. "Elizabeth, you've got to calm down. Are you sure you've checked every possible place she could be? Over."

Taking a deep breath to steady herself, she repeated step by step her efforts to find the missing young woman.

The missionary pilot listened, a sinking feeling in the pit of his stomach. "Elizabeth, listen to me. I want you to look again, slowly and carefully. Check the entire house and the village. Ask questions of the natives. We have to know for sure she's not there before I notify the authorities and home base in Dallas. Do you understand me? Over."

"I understand. I'll ask every native in the village and look in every nook and cranny of this house. Pete, pray that I'm wrong, and she's here somewhere. Over."

"Will do. You let me know when you're sure one way or the other. Over."

"I will. Foothills Mission House, over and out." She turned away from the radio and, with renewed determination, began to methodically search every room of the house. She gave the same thorough inspection to the outside areas before returning to the village.

Repeating her questions to the natives, she received the same response. The young foreigner had gone back up the hill toward the mission house in the late afternoon. Elizabeth ran her hands through her hair, shaking her head. "But she never came back to the mission house. Surely someone saw where she went."

News that their new missionary was lost had spread rapidly through the village, bringing the natives running to surround Elizabeth, their voices raised in a babble of questions.

"Please, I need your help." With upraised arms she signaled for quiet. "Does anyone know where Sierra went after she headed toward the mission house?" She put a hand to her mouth, looked over the sea of dark faces, and waited hopefully. Feeling a tug on her clothing, Elizabeth glimpsed down to find an angelic little face looking up at her.

"Sariase knows," the little girl said with quiet assurance.

All eyes focused on the child. Elizabeth knelt beside her. "What did you see? Tell me Sariase," she implored, grasping the child by her shoulders with gentleness.

"See her go jungle." She pointed toward the verdant mass, and her large dark brown eyes were solemn.

"Where? Which trail?" Elizabeth responded.

Taking the white woman's hand, the small girl led her to the trail down which Sierra had disappeared. "She go here."

Elizabeth pondered the implications of this new information and wondered what to do next. To go off into the jungle by herself in search of the missing young woman was out of the question. As if in answer to the dilemma, her native language helper stepped forward.

"You stay here. We'll go look." He indicated several of the village men.

"Oh, thank you Kito. Please hurry. I'll wait here and pray very hard that she's all right." Time seemed to drag intolerably as she waited for the search party to return.

After what seemed like hours, they came through the curtain of green at a fast trot. The timeworn wrinkles of Kito's face gathered into grave lines when he approached the missionary woman. "We have found footprints by the orchid pool."

"Can you show me?"

With a nod he turned back into the jungle with Elizabeth following close behind.

Elizabeth's hand tightened on the radio microphone. "They were Sierra's footprints, Pete! There's no doubt in my mind. And they were surrounded by at least a dozen barefoot men's prints. They headed straight up the mountain. She's been taken captive!" She was so frightened by what she had seen at the pool that she forgot radio etiquette, her words hung empty in the air.

"Okay, there's no doubt about it then. Josh and James will be there anytime now. Tell them to call me as soon as they get there. I'm going to call the authorities right now. We need to pray, like we've never prayed before. I don't have to tell you what it'll do to Josh if something has happened to her. Over and out."

Elizabeth stared at the microphone, then sank to her knees and turned her face toward heaven as tears streamed from her eyes. "Father, please protect Sierra. Don't let any harm come to her. And please bring James to me now. I need him." As if in answer, the front door opened and she heard her husband's voice.

"Lizbeth, where are you? What's going on? There's a big uproar in the village. Are you all right?"

"James, thank God you're home." She flung herself into the arms of her husband and clung tightly.

"There, there, darling. It's all right. I'm here now." He held her close and stroked her back in gentle reassurance. "Tell me what's happened."

"Oh James, it's all my fault. You left her with me, and now she's gone." Rivers of tears ran down her face. "It's Sierra, she's…"

Pounding feet and a slamming door interrupted her. The two looked up to find their son standing in the doorway, his face white and eyes blazing.

CHAPTER 20

"Pete, I need Jonti." Josh said, his hand tightening on the microphone. "He's the best tracker I know. Tell him what's happened and to come as soon as possible. Over."

"He's on his way, buddy. I called him soon as Elizabeth confirmed Sierra's disappearance. I haven't been able to notify Dr. Cook because of the time difference, but I'll be calling him next. Are you headed out to start the search? Over."

"Affirmative. Kito and some of the best trackers in the village are going with me. Over."

"Cheryl and I are praying for you and that little gal, buddy. Black Hills Mission Station. Over and out."

"Foothills Mission House, over and out."

Josh stared at the small shoe prints surrounded by the dozen or more pairs of bare footprints. His stomach knotted. He had warned her not to go into the jungle alone. Guilt washed over him. He realized in showing her this beautiful spot, he may have inadvertently led her to her death. Quick on that thought came denial.

"Tuan Josh." Kito said, he and Yamo, one of the best trackers in the village, had been looking at the ground. "We see something strange here. These prints," he said, and pointed to round depressions in the soft earth, "are not footprints. These prints are made by knees. They on their knees before the missionary lady. Also, there's no blood by the lady's prints. We think the young lady is not hurt."

"But for how long?" Josh said, and put both hands to his head, pushing against the dark thoughts that threatened to overwhelm him. "We must find her and soon."

Raphael looked at the knee-prints in the dirt and frowned. He knew that natives, even very primitive natives, only exhibit attitudes of worship when they believe they're in the presence of a god. He wondered why they would think that of the young woman and came to the conclusion that they wouldn't unless they saw an angelic being. But he knew that Zephon would only reveal herself in her angelic form under dire circumstances. He flew slowly over the area, looking for clues. At the back of the clearing a wisp of sulphurous stench made him fly close to the ground in search of its source. He found it and touched down quickly, bending one knee to the ground. The stench rose around him, nauseating in its force, and he knew Zephon fought a demon of great power on the spot and won. But he wondered how many demons awaited them in the high jungles.

"Forgive me for interrupting you, Dr. Cook, but there's an emergency call from the Black Hills Mission Station in Irian Jaya."

Dr. Cook looked up from his conversation with Ed when his secretary stuck her head in the door. A look of concern replaced the peaceful smile that was his usual expression. "Excuse me, son. I think I should take this call." Pushing a button, he lifted the receiver on his desk. "Dr. Cook here."

"I'm afraid we have some bad news for you, sir." Pete's voice came across the miles with amazing clarity. "Sierra's disappeared. It seems she went into the jungle alone while James and Josh were down here to pick up a part. All the signs indicate a high mountain tribe abducted her. They've taken her up the mountains. Josh organized a search party, and the authorities have been notified. Jonti's on his way to help with the tracking. We're praying like we've never prayed before. I know I don't need to tell you what this'll do to Josh if she isn't recovered safely, Dr. Cook."

"How long has she been missing?"

"Since yesterday about four or five o'clock our time, Elizabeth thinks. Also, there's no sign she was hurt in any way during the abduction."

"Thank you for notifying me Pete. Please let me know immediately of any new developments. I'll get a prayer chain going and notify Sierra's relatives. Good-by, son." The mission director replaced the receiver and stared at the phone as if lost in thought. After a moment, he rang his secretary and in short precise sentences informed her of the emergency. "Call everyone on the prayer chain and also all of Sierra's supporting churches. Get a chorus of prayer lifted to the Lord as soon as possible." Dr. Cook looked up from his desk to find Ed looking at him with grave eyes.

"Miss Evans is in serious trouble?"

"I'm afraid so Edward, and I could use your help. You've become friends with Sierra's cousin Eleanor, have you not?" At Ed's nod he continued. "I'm going to visit Sierra's grandmother. She's an old and dear friend of mine. It would be of great assistance to me if you could carry the news to Eleanor."

"Of course, Dr. Cook. I'll be glad to help in any way I can."

"Thank you, son. I knew I could count on you. Let's pray before you go."

Eleanor grabbed her purse and headed for the door of her apartment. "An afternoon of shopping is what I need." She had been restless all day, her thoughts kept returning to Sierra. "I miss her. That's the problem. This place is like a morgue, now that she's gone." She stopped at the hallway mirror, checking her appearance as usual before going out.

The face in her mirror was artfully made up. Large amber eyes with thick lashes stared back at her, their warm glow enhanced by the mass of tumbled golden curls that framed her face and hung almost to her waist. The rich brown silk of her blouse made a perfect foil for her eyes and hair. Satisfied that she was presentable, Ellie turned away from her reflection. She opened the door of her apartment. "Oh! Hello."

Edward paused as he reached for the doorbell and stared at her, his brow knit and his hand fell to his side.

"How nice to see you Ed. Please come in." Ellie stepped back, allowing him to enter her apartment. "This is a pleasant surprise." She stopped, realizing he was strangely silent.

Ed was having a hard time gathering his thoughts. He had actually been avoiding Eleanor for sometime because of the way her presence affected him. She was a distraction he felt unable to handle at this point in his life.

The severity of the expression on his face captured her attention, and she had a premonition of doom. "What's wrong? Something's happened. Oh no! It's Sierra. She's in trouble, isn't she?"

"Yes, serious trouble." He nodded, then watched in horror while the poised, self-confident young woman turned whiter than his shirt. Almost in slow motion her eyes closed, and she crumbled toward the floor. He jumped to catch her limp form and carried her to the sofa. "Ellie, Eleanor!" He rubbed her hands repeatedly. "Miss Evans, please wake up!"

Dark lashes fluttered against scary white cheeks. "What...? Oh, I'm sorry. How silly of me." She struggled to sit up, and the color returned to her cheeks in a rush.

"Are you all right? Do you want some water or something?" Edward dragged his eyes away from her, casting them about the room, struggling with his own embarrassment. He took a deep breath and exhaled with force, fighting against the pleasure he felt when holding her in his arms.

"I'm fine. Please tell me what happened to my cousin." She reached for his hand.

"Are you sure you're all right?" He enclosed her fingers in his.

At her affirmative nod, he launched into the story, telling it slowly while watching her reaction. When he finished two large tears slid down her cheeks. She closed her eyes, and a little sob escaped her, wrenching at his heart.

"And she's so far away, there's nothing I can do." Eleanor's said, slumping forward.

"You can pray," Ed replied.

She shook her head and the tears came faster. "It wouldn't do any good for me to pray. I don't even know how to do it properly."

Ed frowned. Then he sat up straighter. He had been so blinded by her physical beauty, he had failed to see the true condition of her soul. *Father forgive me. Help me to share the gospel with her. Please open her heart to your son.* Calmness filled him as he finished the prayer.

"Eleanor, do you want to talk to God and have absolute assurance that he hears you and that Jesus is standing by his father's side pleading your case?"

"Can anyone really know that for sure?"

"God has promised us in his word that there is a way we can be sure, and God always keeps his promises. May I share with you what he says to us?"

"Yes, you need a Bible, don't you?" She opened a cabinet in the end table, producing a volume that looked brand new. Its leather cover was a delicate shade of mauve rose, and the silver gilt pages matched Eleanor's name that was inscribed on the cover.

"This is beautiful," Ed commented, and took the book from her hands.

"Thank you. Sierra gave it to me for my last birthday. She made me promise to read it sometimes. I'm afraid I haven't kept that promise. The few times I've tried, I either found it very confusing or it put me to sleep." She explained sheepishly.

Ed smiled at her, finding her honesty refreshing. He opened the pages of God's word and began to share his faith with her. "In Romans, chapter three, verse twenty-three, it says that all have sinned and fallen short of the glory of God. And in Isaiah 59:2, it explains that sin separates us from God. Romans 6:23 tells us that the penalty for sin is death. But Jesus died to pay the penalty; that's in 1 Peter 3:18 and he wants us to trust him and be saved, according to Ephesians 2:8-9." He turned the pages of the Bible to each of the scriptures and showed them to her.

Eleanor found herself really listening as the kind young man read portions of the scriptures to her and explained each of them. She felt something strange happening to her heart as she listened; it was as though she was hearing it for the first time, and it made sense to her.

"And God says in Revelation 3:23, 'Behold, I stand at the door and knock, if anyone hears my voice and opens the door, I will come in to him, and will dine with him, and he with me.' The door he is knocking on is the door of your heart. All you have to do is open the door and let him in. He wants to be part of your life. But he won't force you; it's your choice. Will you let him in?" Ed waited, barely daring to breathe after he asked for her decision.

"If I say yes, I'll have to give up my way of life, won't I?" she asked, hesitating.

Ed smiled. He saw that she wanted to say yes. "In Acts 3:19, He says we're to change our mind and attitude to God and turn to him, so He can cleanse away our sins. Eleanor, I promise you, having him in your heart will enrich your life so much, you won't even miss anything you choose to give up."

She saw by the honest expression in his eyes that he truly believed everything he had been sharing with her. And he was right, there was a summons going on inside her. *Come on Ellie, say yes, please say yes!* She seemed to hear Sierra's voice in her mind. "Yes, I will let him in. What do I need to do?"

Ed exhaled, and a weight like eternity lifted from his chest. He grabbed her hands and squeezed them as he led her in the prayer of faith and then in a petition for the safety of her cousin.

Ramiel watched his charge lead the young woman to Christ and rejoiced. He looked around the room, eager to welcome the guardian of God's new child. His eyes lit up and he raised a hand in greeting when his good friend, Kaylion, sailed through the ceiling and landed by Eleanor's side.

"I want to tell someone," Eleanor said, and stood up. "Oh, I wish Sierra were here, so I could tell her. My grandmother! That's who I can tell. Ed, will you come with me to my grandmother's house? I want you to meet her. She'll be so happy for me. Oh no! I'll have to tell her about Sierra."

Ed smiled at this evidence of her conversion, and shook his head. "She should know by now. Dr. Cook went to tell her."

"Then she needs me. Will you come with me please?" Her smile had a special radiance as she seemed to glow with an inner light.

"I'll come with you to your grandmother's, if you'll come with me to church on Sunday." He heard himself say.

"Deal." She extended her hand.

He took it, realizing that his life just became a lot more complicated.

CHAPTER 21

Sierra put one foot in front of the other automatically. Her mind felt almost numbed by the exhaustion of her body. They had been climbing for three days, further and further up the mountain, until now they could look down on the clouds. She recited scripture and prayed without ceasing in order to calm her fears as they left the civilized world far behind. Her captors had been kind, but they seemed determined to reach their village now, so they pressed on, even though she knew they must see her tiredness. She was sure they must have reached an extremely high altitude after all the climbing, and she felt her lungs were about to burst from the exertion, but the natives moved relentlessly on. With a burst of energy, they increased their pace yet again, reminding her of Grandma Charlotte's old mule when he sensed the barn was near. Sierra smiled at the memory, and then she realized that they might also be near the natives' village.

Zephon had kept up her surveillance during the trek up the mountain, watching for the reappearance of the enemy. On the second day, in the dusk of evening, she spotted the witch doctor, following in their trail. He stayed well behind the last native in line, furtive and ominous in his secretive movements. She dared not fly closer, lest she let Sierra out of her vision, but she wanted to check for the presence of the powerful demon. Something told her he was there; he would return to a vacant house, and bring an evil horde with him.

They came over a rise. The ground leveled out as they entered a high mountain valley, and the jungle opened up before Sierra's eyes. A small bubbling river ran through a green meadow that was a buzz of activity. Natives seemed to emerge from the ground itself, and she realized with amazement that their homes were mounds built into the side of the mountain, hugging the earth until they seemed part of it. The flow of humanity assembled into a huge crowd, but the curious onlookers parted when the warriors came forward with their captive. Gasps of awe and whispers ran through the crowd. Many gestured towards her, but the hisses from others made her want to hide from them all.

Tohnii led his captive to an immense tree that towered over a large grass covered mound in the center of the village. A white headed man, whose dark face bore the wrinkles of many years, was seated in front of the manhouse, before the throng. Scarlet and gold feathers decorated his cape and headdress, and the top of the long staff in his hand. A pendant of colorful and intricate design hung around his neck.

Sierra's eyes opened wide. The ornament on his chest depicted a blazing sunrise in shades of vermilion on an azure sky. The old man lifted the ornament and gazed a long time at the brightly colored symbol, then he raised eyes as black as a moonless night to compare the vision before him to the ancient ornament.

Tohnii stepped forward and, with dignity befitting the momentous occasion, introduced them. She had been abducted by Tohnii, who, judging by his resemblance, could only be the son of Sawahii, the old man before her, and Sierra knew before her captor finished, Sawahii was the chief of the Kai.

The chief beckoned to Sierra, and she moved forward, but with an ear-splitting screech, the skull-crowned native from the orchid pool rushed past her and flung his misshapen form between her and the chief. Tohnii rammed his spear toward the witchdoctor's face.

Zephon drove her sword into the nearest small demon at the same moment. The demon-driven man raised gnarled hands in mock surrender while the powerful demon leered at Zephon from his perch on the man's back.

Verbal chaos reigned. The witchdoctor and Tohnii hurled insults at each other, their voices filled with angry sneers, until with one word, Sawahii commanded silence. He spoke to his son in what could only be a rebuke and then turned to the witchdoctor, addressing him as Quilpii.

Sierra's quick glimpse of the witchdoctor at the orchid pool in no way prepared her for her first close view of him. He rocked back and forth atop crooked legs, while hissing and casting venomous looks toward Sierra. She shivered from the malice that glittered in his red-rimmed eyes. He saw her fear and leaned toward her until she saw every pore in his grotesque and distorted face, and smelled his fetid breath when he hissed threats of torture and death. Sierra recoiled, and the witchdoctor smiled victoriously, turned and spoke to the chief at length, making threatening gestures towards her.

Sierra knew he asked for her death. Unable to look into the evil she saw in his face, she closed her eyes and tried to pray, but shivers racked her body, and her mind refused to focus. Only a feeble cry for help formed in her mind. She realized the witchdoctor had stopped his loud demands, and Sawahii was speaking to his son.

Tohnii answered his father in slow and careful speech and looked at her frequently. Sierra knew he wanted her to understand him. He made gestures along with his words, and he seemed to be telling Sawahii about the encounter at the orchid pool.

Sierra tried to follow the story, but several key phrases eluded her. She thought he said that the natives saw someone with her at the pool, but the description of the person made no sense. Besides, she had been alone, so she thought that she must have misunderstood him.

But while Tohnii spoke, the chief sat up straighter, and he looked at her for a very long time, then at the witchdoctor. When his son finished speaking, Sawahii remained silent, looking from Sierra to the witchdoctor for long moments. Finally he raised his staff, pounded the shaft on the ground, and spoke with finality.

The witchdoctor hissed, raised a clenched fist toward her, and stomped away.

She was their prisoner. Tohnii or another guard followed her wherever she went.

Sawahii summoned her daily to his presence, and then he sat looking expectantly at her. The witchdoctor sat by his side, and the menace in his bloodshot eyes signaled a boiling anger that threatened to spill over in violence at any opportunity. Removed from Quilpii's umbrella of evil, Sierra prayed hard, knowing instinctively that the hand of God was the only thing that stood between her and the witchdoctor's vengeance.

Zephon stood by Sierra with her sword raised, ready to ward off any attack, and stared the demons down. The smaller demons cowered before her, hiding their blackened and distorted faces from the light. But the powerful demon spread his great vulture wings, sneered at her, and extended an arm, beckoning to her with sharpened talons. "Come little angel. Let's test the power of your arm. We're in my territory now." He croaked from a raspy throat, and his words hung in a rotten egg stench around him.

Refusing to comply, Zephon stood her ground. She felt the absence of Sierra's prayer when the witchdoctor was near, and another essential voice was missing also. Zephon looked at Sierra, saw the struggle within her, and wondered how long they could hold out against such evil.

Sierra knew what Sawahii wanted, but she was unable to communicate well enough to tell him about the God who loved him. Never before had she wanted to learn a language as badly as she wanted to learn the language of the Kai. Not only for their sake but for all the people who loved her and must be worried about her safety. Sierra spent every possible moment studying the language. Its musical intonations were not unlike the language of the McCabe's village. She was absolutely jubilant when she began to piece together small phrases, but then she seemed to hit a plateau in her learning curve and discouragement set in.

Over a week had passed since her abduction, and Sierra walked back toward her hut, after a visit with Sawahii, feeling overwhelmed by the strangeness of her surroundings. Every day had brought a stronger wave of homesickness. She missed her grandmother, Eleanor, Dr. Cook, and the McCabes; but more than all the rest, she longed for Josh. His face was like a flame in her mind that burned brighter with every passing day. She knew she suffered from culture shock, so she tried to focus on the things which were similar, few though they were. The love the people had for their children, and their sense of family provided anchors for her in a sea of unfamiliarity.

And in spite of all her efforts, she still couldn't communicate fully with the people. Her shoulders sagged, and she stared at the pebble-strewn ground with her chin almost on her chest.

When she was alone in her dwelling, she huddled near the fire with her head on her knees, watching the smoke rise towards the smoke hole. Everyday she'd prayed for strength and help from God, asking him why she couldn't pray when near Quilpii, but her prayers seemed to vanish like the smoke against the gray sky. *God help me. I can't do this on my own.* She sat with her eyes closed after her prayer, surrounded by the smoky woodsy smell of the bamboo and mud walls, and then she felt a presence near her.

Sierra's eyes snapped open. A young woman sat beside her. Her features startled Sierra. Although dark like a native, her bone structure was entirely different, and her eyes radiated joy. Goosebumps flew down Sierra's arms with the uncanny feeling that she knew the girl, but she realized that it was impossible.

The young woman placed a gentle hand on Sierra's arm and said, "My name's Zephon. Be at peace. You have friends here."

Every afternoon when Sierra was along in her hut, Zephon came to visit her. They talked for hours, and Sierra realized that communicating in the Kai language with Zephon was much easier than with anyone else. She never saw Zephon during her walks through the village, but she assumed that her new friend went with the other women into the forest every day to gather food. Sierra's depression lifted. Under Zephon's tutelage, she began to learn the Kai language at a much faster pace, and with every passing day, her prayers while near Quilpii grew stronger.

"We have lost the trail, my friend, and something feels wrong in the jungle" Jonti said, and stopped walking. He looked around, his eyes flitting from one side of the jungle to another, his body tense as a drawn bow. "The rain has completely obliterated all trace of their passing. Only a miracle from God can help us find her now."

Raphael and Ithuriel nodded in agreement, but they knew that more than one miracle was needed. The darkness of the morning came from more than the clouds. Shadows gathered. Hiding in the mist and behind the foliage, they crept nearer.

Raphael felt their influence on his charge and touched his sword hilt; it droned, increasing in resonance with every passing second.

"The prayer cover increases," Ithuriel said, and smiled in anticipation.

"Yes." Raphael nodded. "He will be here soon." Raphael saw the struggle in his charge, and recognized that it came from within, and from the demons that stealthily crept closer. He wanted to drive them away, but he knew the time was not ripe.

Josh stared at the ground in abject misery, refusing to admit that his friend's words echoed his own thoughts. They were alone in the forest, the other trackers had given up and gone back to their normal lives days before. The traitorous rain continued to fall, but its torrential flow had slowed to drizzle, weeping from the trees in broken streams. *Sierra's dead.* The whispered words haunted him, and twisted his heart, feeding his anger at God.

Jonti frowned at the face of his friend where dark circles rimmed haunted eyes in a countenance as gaunt as death. Josh had pushed them both to the limits of their endurance; and for love, Jonti had followed without complaint, knowing he would have felt the same if Kimi were in Sierra's place. And now for love, he must be honest. Jonti had listened to the prayers of everyone in Irian Jaya who loved Sierra, but one voice was noticeably silent. "Josh, my friend, you must ask God. Only he can help you to find her."

Sierra's dead. The evil warriors whispered, and surged toward

Josh, one daring to lay a claw on his head.

In an instant, the angels drew their swords and collided with the cloud of demons. Brilliant streaks of light flashed from Raphael's and Ithuriel's swords, ripping a hail of shrieks from the wounded demons.

Raphael fought to reach Josh. Bellowing, he surged forward, then spinning to avoid a red blade, he brought his sword around in a white-hot arc to mow down a mass of demons. But more appeared.

Laughing at Raphael's efforts, the demon of anger tightened his grip on Josh.

"No, the fault, it's God's." Josh wrenched the words out. "The danger, the danger she's in. For this, he's to blame." His mouth twisted, he turned on Jonti with clenched fists. "Why does he take away the people I love? What does he want from me, Jon?" The words spurted from him, a geyser of anger.

"He wants you to trust that his way is best always, in all circumstances. He wants you to surrender your will to him, my friend. He wants all of you, my brother, every part of your brain and your heart. Pray, Josh, pray."

"No!" Josh grabbed his head with both hands. "I can't forgive him for what he's done to my family, Jon," Josh said, and his shoulders hunched. "He betrayed our trust and our love by letting Michael and Sarah die."

Raphael heard the demon's laugh, and he clapped his wings downward and shot into the sky, seeking a new avenue of access to his charge.

The demon loosened his hold on Josh, startled by the sudden move from Raphael.

But He saved you Josh. A gentle voice insisted in his mind.

Josh shook his head against the memory of the hand that thrust him from the bottom of the river. "And now he's taken Sierra away from us too. Why Jon? Tell me why!"

"I do not know all the answers, my friend." Jon put his hand on Josh's shoulder. "But it may help if you see them as a gift. God blessed you with a wonderful brother and sister to love. They enriched your life, and you wanted the joy of their presence to go on and on, but God needed them to come home. He gave them to you for little while, and it was his right to take them back. Sierra may not be lost to you. I feel it in my heart; if you ask God to keep her safe and bring her back, he will. But *you* must do the asking. Let's talk to Him, Josh, together, like we did when we were kids." Jonti raised his voice and hands to heaven.

Raphael saw an opening by Josh, but then the demons closed ranks, raising their swords like a field of crimson wheat. Tension filled the air, like an overfilled balloon ready to explode, and then Raphael heard the trumpet.

The demons shrieked, raising their distorted faces to the sky, and what they saw sent most of them scattering in all directions.

An angel of enormous proportions hovered over the clearing, his wings reflecting the light of a million diamonds.

"Michael," Raphael and Ithuriel shouted, cheered, and rushed toward Josh, where only one evil minion still whispered. Raphael's sword punctured the demon's chest, ending the evil whisper in a choked gargle, and the imp disappeared in a puff of smoke.

The anger in Josh's heart expanded like a festering wound, causing pain and pressure until he felt his very insides tearing apart in a fight for lordship of his life. It had been so long since he had talked to God. Even when he knew he was drowning in the river, he'd refused to ask for help, but God had saved him; he knew that now. Great gulping sobs shook him as he lifted his head to the sky. "God. Help me. I can't do this on my own." Tears melted from his eyes, joining the rain on his cheeks to release all the pent-up pain that had darkened his way for years.

Jonti embraced his friend and held him, praying silently for complete healing of his wounds. Like a storm that has been building in intensity, and at its peak is a testimony to the power of God, was Josh's surrender.

Josh fell to his knees, head bowed. "God, please, forgive me. I've been a stubborn, hardheaded, fool. Help me to yield my will to yours. And Lord, if it be your will, bring Sierra back to me. Don't take her out of my life. Protect her please. Keep her safe."

"Precious Father in heaven, give us a sign that Sierra is all right," Jonti whispered.

As Jonti finished the plea for reassurance, Josh felt the warmth of the sun on his face. It broke through the clouds bathing the freshly washed forest in gold.

"Look!" Jonti shouted, and lifted his arm.

At his friend's exclamation, Josh turned toward the mountaintop to see a magnificent rainbow, its colors a brilliant arch against the misty sky. "It's the sign you asked for Jon. She's all right, and what's more. That's where she is. There!" He indicated the rainbow's end. "The valley between the two mountain tops. That's where she is. I know it!"

With renewed determination, the two friends headed up the trail again. The cleft between the mountains was their landmark as they pushed on toward their goal.

Raphael and Ithuriel saluted the departing archangel, then joined their charges, rejoicing that the prodigal son had come home.

Chapter 22

Sawahii sat between his son and Quilpii and looked solemnly at the young foreign woman. The guards he had set to watch over her gave good reports on this one. She spent many hours practicing their language, and she was kind to everyone in the village, from the smallest child to the oldest wise one of the Kai. Everyday he called her to his presence and asked the same question, and everyday she had looked at him with non-comprehension of his words. Today, again, her forehead was knit in concentration, and he knew she waited expectantly. In deep tones of great age, he repeated the question. "Are you the one of the legend? The lady of the dawn who will tell us of the one true God?"

A wave of incredible relief washed over Sierra, and she clapped her hands as she realized that she understood him. "Praise God, yes! If it's God's will, I'm the one. EE-Taow, it is true."

The face of the old chief creased into a thousand wrinkles as he smiled and chortled with glee, pounding the ground with his staff. "Tell me of the one true God." It was not a question this time, but a command.

Quilpii jumped up from his seat with a shriek that lifted the birds from the trees, their cries piercing the jungle. "The spirits are angry," he said, pointing to the noisy flock. "They will punish us if we do not kill her." He rubbed his hands together and bared his teeth at Sierra, his voice rising, "They wants us to kill her, Sawahii, they wants," he screeched, and flung himself at Sierra, but Tohnii stopped him with the point of his spear.

Zephon's blade made quick work of the lesser demons, and they scurried into the jungle like frightened rats, dragging their wounded limbs, but the captain of evil snarled in defiance and sank his claws even deeper into his victim.

"Ahhh! Ahhh! They begin," Quilpii wailed and clawed at his back, twisting and writhing.

Sierra recoiled from the evil she sensed in him, and then compassion overcame her revulsion. She dared not touch him, but she felt compelled to pray. "Evil spirits, be gone in the name of Jesus. I command you by the power invested in me in Christ to leave him, and don't return."

"Yes! It's about time," Zephon said with a smile. Spinning like a tornado, her blade traced brilliant arcs, then she heaved her sword and hewed her demon opponent's legs from his body. With a horrendous scream, he exploded in a stream of red smoke that spiraled away into the trees.

The witchdoctor tried to run, but Tohnii stopped him with the spear to his throat. Without taking his eyes from his captive, the chief's son spoke to his father. "Shall I bleed Quilpii like a pig and feed him to the buzzards?"

"No! Please!" Sierra stepped forward and touched the chief, then clapped her hands to her mouth in horror at her breach of etiquette. "Forgive me Sawahii. But please don't kill him. God says we are to forgive our enemies and even pray for them." When the chief and Tohnii still looked bent on retribution, she grasped at the one thing she knew might convince them. "The legend says I'm to tell the Kai people of the one true God. That means all of them, even Quilpii." She nodded toward the quivering man.

"He must be punished." Sawahii insisted.

"Then punish him by making him learn about God."

The chief raised his eyebrows, adding to the wrinkles on his forehead as he pondered her suggestion, then he said, "It is good. He will listen. Tell us of the one true God." He took a seat and motioned for them to do likewise.

Whispering a prayer for assistance, Sierra began. Choosing her words with great care, she told them of the God who is all powerful, but who loves all men so much that he sent his own son to die for them. Breaking through the clouds, the sun trembled through the tree leaves, stealing in among the branches to shine long paths of light. The birds returned and perched in the tree overhead, adding their song to her voice.

Communicating in the new language still presented a challenge for her. After a while, she found herself exhausted from the effort. Sawahii sensed her tiredness and signaled that she was dismissed.

Sierra wanted to stay. She needed desperately to make him understand that she must return to the mission house. James and Elizabeth and Josh must be told that she was all right. But she knew from observing the customs of the culture that when the chief dismissed someone, they must immediately leave his presence.

Day after day, the pattern continued. Sawahii directed their conversation, Tohnii joined them, whenever hunting duties allowed him time, and Quilpii listened, his eyes a little brighter with interest each day. Whenever Sierra tried to bring up the subject of her leaving the Kai, the chief dismissed the suggestion as out of the question. His curiosity and questions about God seemed never ending. Sierra began with the creation and told him every Bible story she could remember.

With each passing day, she knew a burning desire to have her Bible from which to teach them. She had searched her heart, remembering her talk with Elizabeth, and found that Josh was right; guilt had been her original motive for being a missionary, but after spending time with the Kai people something new had replaced it—love. And she knew without a doubt that God had brought her there to be their Bible translator; she must help them put God's word in their language.

She must convince the chief that she could not tell them everything there is to know of God unless she had her Bible. Sierra's mind wrestled with the dilemma, and she wondered how to explain to a stone-age tribe that there is a book about God? The task seemed almost impossible. The Kai culture contained no written language, and they seemed to have no words to explain the concept of words.

Sawahii pounded his staff on the ground, demanding that Sierra respond to his request to tell him more about Jesus.

She sat in silence, eyes closed, deft to his question. Her thoughts were a prayer as Sierra asked for guidance. *Father in heaven, please, help me to explain to him about your word. Give me a way to make him understand. In Jesus' name, amen.* She lifted her head and looked at the aged one. "There are many more stories about the one true God, but I can't tell them to you."

The old chief bristled, affronted by what he believed was a refusal to share. "Why will you not tell Sawahii more?"

"The stories are not here," she said and pointed to her head, "or here," and to her heart. "They are at the mission house."

"No!" He shook his head, believing this to be just another attempt on her part to leave the Kai.

"It is truth!" She reached out to him. "There are so many stories I can not remember them all. They are…" She said and stopped, unable to find the words in his language to explain. "There must be a way." She sighed and pushed her hair back, staring at his face. In frustration her eyes fell from his obsidian gaze to rest on the ornament that symbolized the Kai. "A symbol," she whispered, "Of course, the answer has been in front of me all the time." Reaching out, she pointed toward the ornament, asking for its name in Kai.

Sawahii lifted the necklace and spoke a Kai word that was new to her.

Sierra's heartbeat accelerated, and she leaned forward as she realized that this could be the answer to her prayer. "The one true God gave my people many 'tokaia'," she said, using the word he had spoken. "They tell us much about him, and he wants my people to share the 'tokaia' with your people. But I have to return to my people to get the 'tokaia'." She held her breath.

He received her words in silence and searched her face, looking deeply into her eyes as if to ascertain the truth. After what seemed like an eternity, he spoke. "You will return soon?" It was not a command. It was a request spoken from the heart of a man who has lived many years and knows he will not live many more.

"I will return soon." The words were a promise, and Sierra knew that, God willing, she must keep it.

Satisfied by her answer, Sawahii issued an order to Tohnii. Turning to Sierra, he looked long into her face again before speaking. "Return to us soon, lady of the dawn."

"Wait!" Quilpii said, and held up his hand. "Do not leave, or the evil spirits will return. I do not want them. I want to be free." He held out his hands to her.

Tears sprang to her eyes. "It's not me who makes you free. It's Jesus. Do you remember that I told you he died to pay for our sins?"

All of the men nodded.

"Do you believe that it is truth?"

A chorus of EE-Taow sounded from the three men. Than Sawahii spoke, "We have seen the power of the one true God."

"And the forgiveness," Quilpii added.

Sierra blinked back the tears. She knew she was witnessing a miracle—the first Christians among the Kai. "If you ask Jesus to come live in your hearts, he will, and he will protect you from the evil spirits. Do you want to do this?"

They all nodded.

"Praise God," Sierra whispered, and lifted her hands toward heaven. "Then ask him."

Sawahii spoke first, then Tohnii, and last of all Quilpii, who raised his head after talking to God and said, "My heart is like a feast."

Zephon clapped her hands and sang in celebration, and then she soared into the sky to greet the new guardians.

Wiping the tears from her eyes, Sierra turned to the chief. "Sawahii, before I leave, I'd like to thank the young woman who came to my hut every afternoon and helped me learn your language. Her name is Zephon. Where could I find her?" She looked from one face to another as silence greeted her question.

"No one among the Kai bears that name," Sawahii answered with a puzzled shake of his head, and the other men agreed.

"Are you sure?" Sierra frowned. "She has soft curls to her shoulders, radiant brown eyes, and she's about this tall." She held her hand out, and then she seemed to hear an echo in her memory, and an "Oh my" in English escaped her. "Fawn? Zephon?" She whispered.

"I have seen her. When we came for you," Tohnii said, his dark eyes large.

"I too." Quilpii struck his chest.

"By the orchid pool?" Sierra looked from one to the other in wonder.

"Yes." Tohnii nodded. "She was in the air above you with wings and a blade like lightning, and then she disappeared."

"Yes," Quilpii added, "she drove the demons away."

"Oh my." Sierra smiled, and then she laughed and raised her hands toward heaven again. "Praise God. Thank you Jesus."

"Is she a god?" Tohnii asked.

"No. I believe she's an angel, my guardian angel. Remember I told you about the angels Gabriel and Michael?"

The men nodded and recounted bits of the stories.

"God has thousands of angels, and some of them serve as guardians and protectors of his children. God tells us in his word that his angel encamps around those who reverence God, and he helps them. God also tells us that all angels are ministering spirits. I believe that all God's children have guardians. You just became God's children when you asked Jesus into your hearts. That means you each have one too."

The three men turned all around, looking up into the sky.

Sierra smiled and hurried to explain. "Normally, we can't see angels. They live in regions beyond our senses. God gave us all a special blessing in allowing us to see her." *Thank you, God, for giving me the most special blessing of all. She ministered to me, and I spoke with her. Thank you Jesus. And thank you for these dear people. Help me to return to them.* With a full heart and eyes, Sierra looked at the chief. "I must teach you one more thing before I go. I must teach you to pray. Praying is talking to God. He wants us to talk to him about everything. Like this." She bowed her head. "Precious Father in heaven. Thank you for the Kai. Keep them safe and help me to return to them. Help Sawahii, Tohnii, and Quilpii to tell everyone in the tribe about you. And help them to pray. For Jesus sake because he died for them. Amen." She lifted her head and looked at Sawahii, "May I go now?"

He nodded and laid his hand on her head in blessing. "Return to us soon, lady of the dawn."

The trek down the mountain began immediately, as though the ancient chief knew he had no time to waste. Happiness made the trail fly by beneath her feet as she followed Tohnii and the small band of warriors down the mountain.

They had been walking for several hours, only stopping briefly to eat when Tohnii raised his hand, halting them, and signaling for silence. He turned his head, and listened. With a few quick commands, the warriors melted into the surrounding jungle, taking Sierra with them. Tohnii motioned for silence again, and then focused his eyes on the trail.

The trail was empty. She listened and heard nothing; an unusual silence reigned in the forest. The birds and small animals were strangely quiet as though they sensed the presence of something unknown to them.

The warriors tensed, and then Sierra heard a voice that sent her heart soaring. With a reflex action she grabbed the arm of Tohnii when he began to lift his weapon. "No! Friends." Before he could stop her, she flung herself from the cover of the foliage and into the view of the man who had just emerged onto the trail.

"Josh!" She rushed towards him.

"Sierra, thank God!" He enfolded her in his arms, holding her as if he would make her a part of him. "Thank you God, thank you."

Tohnii watched from the shadows long enough to see that his task was completed. He had returned the lady of the dawn to her people. With a silent signal, he and his warriors vanished into the jungle.

As if in a trance of happiness, Sierra heard Josh thanking God for her safety. She cupped his face in her hands and held his gaze. "Did I hear you praising God?" His dark green eyes shimmered with love and something else. She gasped, realizing the sorrow was gone.

With a little smile that tugged at her heart he nodded. "I've made peace with God, Sierra." He paused for just a moment before continuing. "Will you marry me?"

She closed her eyes wanting to savor the moment and hold it forever.

Josh knew a moment of fear as he thought she would say no.

"You have no idea how much I want to say yes." She stopped, and his face beamed at her words. "I have so much to tell you. But first I have to tell you about the promise I just made to the Kai. I promised I would return with God's word and share it with them, and I fully intend to keep that promise, if God is willing. I have to tell you also that you were right about the guilt, but it's gone now Josh. God replaced it with love for those people, and they need to know Him. I can't marry you unless you're willing to help me keep the promise."

He hugged her to him. "I love you, and I would follow you anywhere, even to a mountain top in Irian Jaya. But why are you so sure that you're the one who's meant to go to the Kai?"

"The Kai! Wait," she said, and held up a finger, "I need to thank Tohnii and his men." She started to turn back up the trail.

Jonti stopped her with a hand to her shoulder. "They are gone already."

"Oh. Why did they leave so soon?" She wondered out loud.

Josh took her hands. "They knew they were no longer needed. You were saying?" He gave her a gentle smile.

She raised a hand and caressed his cheek, wondering at the thinness. "Because all of my life when God wants to make sure I get the message, he tells me from three sources. Jonti's grandmother called me the lady of the dawn," she said, and smiled at Josh's friend. "Sawahii, the chief of the Kai, called me by the same title."

"But that's only two." Josh looked puzzled.

She smiled. "Remember my secret?"

He nodded.

"My parents make the third source, and God had a hand in it there also. I was born at sunrise in the Sierra Madre Mountains of Mexico. My parents named me Dawn, Sierra Dawn. When I was a kid, my dad called me lady of the dawn."

Jonti laughed at the expression on Josh's face. "Let's go, my friend. My lady is waiting for me." Clapping him on the back, he started down the mountain.

THE END